Also by Phil Earle

Storey Street

Demolition Dad

For older readers

Being Billy

Saving Daisy

Heroic

Bubble Wrap Boy

For younger readers

Albert and the Garden of Doom

Elsie and the Magic Biscuit Tin

Phil Earle

SUPERHERO STREET

Illustrated by Sara Ogilvie

Orion
Children's Books

ORION CHILDREN'S BOOKS

First published in Great Britain in 2016 by Hodder and Stoughton

1 3 5 7 9 10 8 6 4 2

Text copyright © Phil Earle, 2016
Illustrations copyright © Sara Ogilvie, 2016

The moral rights of the author and illustrator have been asserted.

A CIP catalogue record for this book
is available from the British Library.

ISBN 978 1 4440 1388 7

Printed and bound in Great Britain by Clays Ltd, St Ives plc

The paper and board used in this book are from well-managed forests
and other responsible sources.

MIX
Paper from
responsible sources
FSC® C104740

Orion Children's Books
An imprint of
Hachette Children's Group
Part of Hodder and Stoughton
Carmelite House
50 Victoria Embankment
London EC4Y 0DZ

An Hachette UK Company
www.hachette.co.uk

www.philearle.com
@philearle
www.facebook.com/PhilEarleAuthor
www.hachettechildrens.co.uk

I wrote this book for my amazing mum, *Sweet Neet*, who
continually puts Wonder Woman firmly in the shade ... and to
my youngest son, Stanley. Whether he's BatStan, SuperStan,
SpiderStan or Stan(Lee), he is always my hero.
P.E.

For Jane, Dave, Calum, Freya, Molly and Angus
S.O.

Who's Who in Storey Street...

Dad ➤

Mouse ➤

Mum

The Triplets ➤

The Twins ➤

The Z-List:

Vortex

Dan-Druff

The Skidmark

Cyclots

1

Dark Days and Dark Knights...

Mouse wished with all his heart that his cape wasn't tucked into his undercrackers. It could be argued that, since he was hanging by his fingertips from a splintering branch of an oak tree, ten metres from the ground, he should've been thinking about other things. Like how he hoped this wasn't going to end with him wearing a full body cast. But that was Mouse for you.

Superheroes were never off duty, which was why he'd climbed the tree in the first place. It had started as an elementary mission, the sort any self-respecting crime fighter cuts their teeth on. Wherever there are trees, there are cats that get stuck in them: it's a well-known cliché – I mean, fact – so when Mouse spotted a distressed moggy caught in the boughs of the oak, he had no option but to bring her safely down to earth. If Mouse's super-strength specs had stayed on his face a little longer, he might have noticed that the cat (called Pig-Tiger – even animals have identity problems) wasn't upset at all. Far from it. She was asleep, dreaming of kippers the size of great white sharks.

But superheroes have to be instinctive, like Peter Parker and his Spidey Sense. So, with no thought for his own personal safety (or that of the dozing cat), Mouse shimmied awkwardly up the trunk.

From there, things had gone seriously awry – like the time in Mouse's favourite comic, when Daredevil shoved his red costume in the wash with his best white sheets – because poor Pig-Tiger didn't like being woken from her heavenly dream. She hissed at Mouse with such ferocity and contempt that our hero slipped from the branch, feeling it crack as his fingers grasped desperately. Pig-Tiger was in no mood to offer a helping paw either, and leaped athletically to the ground, landing without a scratch. Mouse's eyesight was lousy without his specs, but he could've sworn the cat smiled at him before strolling off to find a mouse with more brains to terrorise.

'Not again,' Mouse muttered to himself. This sort of thing

wouldn't keep happening if his superpowers would hurry up and kick in. If he could just fly or shoot webs from his wrists, then he'd be on the ground in a flash.

Unfortunately, no matter how many comic books he read, or how many spiders he caught in the hope of one of them biting him with their radioactive teeth, he remained plain old Michael J Mouse, devoid of any real skills, except for the ability to get into dumb situations like this. He was beginning to think that super powers only existed for other people. And boy, that made him sad.

What Mouse didn't realise, though, was that things were about to change. He wasn't destined to stand in the shadows for much longer, disguised as a speccy, awkward ten year old.

Uh-uh, no way, not on your nelly. Within weeks, Mouse would be living the superhero life. Just not in the way he'd dreamed it . . .

The Invisible Mouse

'You can drop me here, thanks, guys,' said Mouse, wincing as his two best pals, Jake and Floss, lowered him onto his doorstep.

'Sure you don't want us to carry you up the stairs?' said Jake.

Mouse blushed and shook his head. He didn't remember Superman ever needing a fireman's lift to his bedroom. It had been embarrassing enough bumping into his friends and needing their help at all. Besides, if the house was in as big a state as it had been when he'd left this morning, he didn't want his mates to see it.

'I'll be fine. Call for me before school tomorrow, though, eh?'

'Maybe I'll bring my dad,' said Jake, beaming. 'He could carry you to the gates with one finger.'

Mouse laughed, despite the pain. It was true – Jake's dad was a man mountain, built like the kind of adversary superheroes faced and defeated every day of their lives. Mouse felt another stab of shame. He couldn't even triumph over a dozing moggie with a dumb name.

Waving to his friends, Mouse pushed open the front door and hobbled in, immediately falling over a small bundle of white fur which whizzed past his ankles.

'Horatio!' he yelled, as the blur shot into the cupboard under the stairs.

Mouse wasn't the only one shouting. Voices bounced from every wall, echoing through the hall and up the stairs. Nonsensical screams and hungry cries. Mouse was used to it. Gripping the wall, he limped down the hallway, adding to the din, 'Muuuuum?'

'In here,' came a sing-song reply, a voice that sounded way too cheerful, given the chaotic racket around her. Mouse stopped at the closed kitchen door, took a long, deep breath, and pushed it open.

WHHHHAAAAAM! The noise engulfed him, blowing his hair back and steaming up his glasses. It was as if a jumbo jet full of trumpeting elephants was using their breakfast table as a runway, except there was neither plane nor elephant to be seen – just a row of five food-splattered high chairs containing the rowdiest bunch of beasts Mouse had ever dreamed of. His brothers.

Yep, the maths is right. I can (despite folk thinking otherwise) count to five, and five there most definitely were. Here, let me prove it.

First, there were the twins: three year olds, Dean and Roger; loud, grizzly, and with an incredible ability to shove more Lego pieces up their noses than would normally fit in a spoiled kid's toy box.

Mouse's dad had cried when he'd found out they were having twins, though Mouse wasn't sure the tears that had splashed down his sequined tuxedo were those of a joyful, expectant father. Mind you, they were nothing in comparison to the tsunami-sized ones that escaped him eighteen months later when he found out they were having triplets as well.

Dad had cried so violently that their neighbours on Storey Street had to wedge sandbags against their front doors. The army hovered outside for two days in canoes, packed with tissues and other essential supplies. Well, that's the version I like to tell anyway . . .

But no amount of tears could stop the twins or the triplets arriving, not from Dad, and not from Mouse either. Before all his brothers came along, Mouse had loved having his mum and dad to himself. Together, they'd build superheroes out of Lego and they'd carry him up and down the stairs like he was flying. Mouse should have guessed, though, as soon as Mum told him the news about even the twins, that this would soon be a thing of the past.

'How are we going to fit everyone in?!' he' d asked when news of the triplets broke, even though that was the least of their concerns. They should've been worrying about ever having a minute to themselves ever again, or how they would ever afford to put six children though university and still afford new animals for Dad's act.

Mum, patient as ever, pointed at her swollen belly and said, 'If I can fit them in here, then we can find space in the house too. Maybe you can move your room up to the attic. You've been on about it for ages.'

Mouse muttered under his breath, despite being secretly pleased about his bedroom. It was still going to be a nightmare, and he wanted Dad and Mum to know it.

'Maybe . . . ' she said, with a grin. 'Maybe you could be more involved this time. Now you're older.'

Mouse's stomach turned at the thought of milky vomit and mustard-coloured poos. He'd seen enough of that with the twins.

'I am NOT changing nappies . . . '

'No, not nappies,' Mum said. 'We were thinking you could help us with names. Three strong names for three strong little brothers.'

It didn't take Mouse long to come up with a definitive shortlist . . .

'Mouse,' Dad barked, 'there is no way in the world we are calling your baby brothers Bat, Spider and Super.'

'Why not? It would be cool. They could all have the same middle name too!'

'But . . . *man* isn't really a name, is it?' Mum said. 'And imagine the mickey-taking at school.'

Mouse was gutted. Why ask him to name the triplets if his suggestion was going to be kicked away? Well, he wasn't going to let it beat him. He was going to come up with acceptable superhero names, even if it killed him.

That was it! He had it. He'd have to do it cleverly, though, so Mum and Dad didn't know what they were agreeing to.

'OK,' he sighed, as if defeated. 'How about *Bruce, Peter* and *Clark?*'

Mum and Dad looked at each other, smiled, then said, 'Nice! And if you like them, so do we. Deal!'

Mouse performed a victory jig as he walked away. Ha! They had no idea that Bruce, Peter and Clark were actually Batman, Spiderman and Superman's alter-ego names! Maybe, just maybe, having five little brothers wasn't going to be as bad as he thought.

Except it was. Of course it was. Do you really think naming

teeny tiny babies after superheroes will make them act like superheroes? Let me tell you, it doesn't work like that.

The only thing the triplets were *super* at was puking, pooing and screaming. Add on top of that the terrible tantrums from Dean and Roger, and, well, Mouse's house was a war zone. Everywhere the eye could see, there was mess – baby toys, wet wipes, nappy bags that smelled so bad Mouse thought a pig

with a belly-ache must have relieved himself in it. There was food splattered over the walls, the floor and even the TV. Judging by how much the five kids cried, the only place there *wasn't* food was in their stomachs!

But somehow Mum seemed to embrace the madness. In fact, she seemed to thrive on it. Mouse would watch in wonder as she simultaneously filled the dishwasher, swept the kitchen floor and fed a wailing baby or five. I know that shouldn't be possible, but it is I tell you, LOOK!!

Such multi-tasking did come at a cost. These days Mum didn't have quite enough eyes to notice *everything* that was going on in Mouse's life, or indeed *anything*. And that hurt him. He thought sadly of the days when her eyes fell only on him. This afternoon, she was so distracted with calming Dean and Roger, while whipping away two of the most toxic nappies known to man, she didn't notice Mouse grabbing a bag of frozen peas for his swollen ankle.

'Did you have a good day, Mouse love?' Mum said without looking up, a dummy between her teeth and a wet wipe in each hand.

'Not really, I've hurt my leg,' he said with a grimace, as he trod on a toy car with his already throbbing foot.

'Tea will be a while yet,' Mum said. She hadn't heard him over Bruce's wails. 'I was hoping your dad might give me a hand. You seen him on your travels?'

Mouse hadn't, but he knew where he'd be. He thought about trying to tell Mum about his day again, getting some sympathy, but then the volume levels from his brothers went mental, and he decided against it.

'I'll find Dad. And if I don't, then I can help,' he sighed.

'Oh, Mouse,' Mum yelled, extracting something truly rancid

from between Bruce's bum cheeks. 'You are a good lad. I promise we'll have some time together later. You can show me that thing you've been talking about.'

'OK,' Mouse answered, knowing full well that the evening would probably end as it always did, with Mum comatose on the floor at the foot of the ladder to his attic room.

But maybe tonight would be different. Maybe Mouse would be able to persuade Dad to help and Mum might actually make it to the attic and onto his bed before she turned into a snoring, dribbling heap. Mouse hopped double-time. Because if he knew Dad, he had his work cut out for him.

The Magic
Wordzzzzzzzzzzzz

Marvin the Magnificent wasn't exactly living up to his name. *Simon the Snorer* would've been more appropriate, or *Colin the Comatose*, or even *Damien the Dribbler*.

It was no surprise to find Dad asleep in the lounge, though Mouse was shocked to see that he hadn't even managed to reach the sofa properly first. His head had found solace on one of its plump cushions, but the rest of his body zig-zagged its way to the floor, contorted into a series of angles more conducive to torture than sleep. Not that it bothered Dad. It didn't bother him that he hadn't removed his work clothes either. His sequined tuxedo shimmered under the lights as his back rose and fell, while his top hat twitched inexplicably on his head.

Ironically, the area around Dad was *full* of life. On the arm of the sofa perched Davina the dove, head held imperiously high, as if disapproving of her master's inability to stay awake. Burrowing

between the sofa cushions was Frederico the rabbit, nibbling the stuffing in a way that had infuriated Mum for years. If he hadn't been such an integral part of Dad's act, Mum would have boiled that bunny years ago.

There were other assorted noises and muffled scurryings going on, especially from Tamara the tarantula, who was dancing her way across the nape of Dad's neck, but Mouse wasn't worried about her. Tamara was completely tame, despite how terrifying she looked.

Mouse carefully removed the top hat from Dad's head and pulled from its murky depths a deep green toad who belched its thanks.

'Don't worry, Reg,' he said, popping the beast into its tank.

'Dad must've been too tired to do the encore tonight. Well, either that or the crowd didn't ask for one.'

That was happening more and more to Marvin the Magnificent, you see. Crowds were so much more difficult to please now. Back in the good old days, the audience would be on their feet, whooping as he finished his act. At least that's what Dad had told Mouse.

'These days I could make a football stadium disappear before their eyes and no one would take their eyes off their phone. I blame the internet,' Dad would moan. 'And Facebook. And that Dynamo fella off the telly and . . . well . . . everything. They're putting me out of business.'

There was some truth in that, sadly. When Mouse was younger, Dad had been top of the bill at the theatre on the seafront. There'd been talk of a tour, TV appearances even. Now though? There were kids' parties and Christmas fêtes, but the only chance of Dad's act appearing on the telly was when Davina perched on

top of it for a rest. She tended to use the screen as a toilet, and Mouse hoped it wasn't a comment on Dad's career prospects.

Mouse felt sorry for his dad. When he'd been in demand, Dad was a different man. He used to lavish gifts on Mouse. He was the one who'd introduced Mouse to comics in the first place, shoving a really rare copy of Batman into his sweaty paws. A comic he'd owned since being a boy himself. He'd been just as generous with Mum. Romantic, too. He'd pull huge bouquets of flowers from his sleeve for her. Mouse remembered he'd once taught Reg the toad to regurgitate a diamond ring. Anything to make her feel special . . .

But now? Poor Marvin had to work harder than ever to put enough food on the table for his kids, so he was always really upset whenever Roger, Dean, Bruce, Peter or Clark flicked it wastefully at the wall. Dad had been spotted licking the wallpaper during one especially work-free month. 'What?' he'd mouthed through a mouthful of puréed broccoli. 'Waste not, want not.'

Day after day he put himself out there – along with the children's parties and Christmas fetes, he went to old people's homes, hospitals and schools – but it seemed his act wasn't quite 'magical' enough to allow him to charge more and work less. By the time he arrived home, he was good for nothing. Well, except collapsing before he could even put his animals back in their cages. Mouse understood it was hard for Dad. But at the same time, he did wish Marvin would pull his finger out and do a *bit* more to help . . .

That reminded him. He should find Cedric the guinea pig. If he blocked Mum's vacuum cleaner again, she'd have him stuffed. Or roast him. He wasn't sure which would be worse. Dutifully, he hobbled round the room chasing down spiders, rabbits and hamsters. It was like being head zoo keeper at the most delinquent petting zoo ever invented. Finally Mouse allowed himself to collapse next to Dad on the sofa, banging his old man's head in the process.

Dad stirred in his sleep. Mouse felt hopeful for a moment. Maybe Dad would wake up and ask him about his day, or even better, go and finally help Mum. But he didn't.

He just rolled over, pulled Mouse into a hug and began to nibble on his ear, whispering, 'Abracadabr—'

'DAD!' Mouse yelled. 'Get off me, will you?!'

Dad awoke with a start. 'Don't make me do the act again!' he yelled. 'They'll eat me alive.'

'It's all right. It's just me. Mum wants you to help with tea.'

'Are the twins in bed yet?' he whispered, voice thick with dread.

'No chance.'

'The triplets?'

'Are you kidding?'

Dad shuddered and loosened his bow tie. 'Tell Mum I'm asleep.' He looked like he wanted to be, more than anything.

'She'll just come and wake you up.'

'Then tell her I'm sick.'

'With what?'

'I don't know. Flu? Typhoid? No, hang on, think of something really contagious. Something I shouldn't go near the twins with, or the triplets.'

'But it's OK for you to give this *thing* to me, is it? Well, thanks!'

Dad blushed, realising how awful it sounded and reached for Mouse's hand. 'I'm sorry, son. I didn't mean it like that. I'm just . . . so . . . tired. If I could get a few hours' unbroken sleep it'll be fine. Think of something to tell Mum, will you? Please? There's a good lad.'

He squeezed Mouse's hand before collapsing back onto the sofa. He was snoring before he reached the cushions.

'Yeah right,' muttered Mouse angrily.

Why couldn't Dad stay awake for one minute and give Mum a hand?

Well he wasn't going to take sides. And besides, Mum had been at work too. All right, so being a lollipop lady wasn't exactly brain surgery, but it was still a job, especially on top of being a full-time mum. Those couple of hours a day were the only times Dad *really* looked after the triplets and twins.

'Is Dad coming?' Mum called from the kitchen. She sounded stressed. Mouse could guess why. Roger and Dean were probably clinging to each of her legs as she nursed Clark and Bruce, while rocking Peter's bouncer with her big toe.

'In a minute,' Mouse yelled back. He knew he should go and

help, but first he wanted to get ice on his ankle. If he didn't, he wouldn't be able to walk tomorrow, and Mum didn't have enough arms to carry him as well. So off Mouse hobbled, up the stairs to his bedroom, with the sad realisation that neither of his loving, but exhausted parents had even noticed there was anything wrong.

Faster than a Speeding Bullet

Mouse's grin stretched wide as the wind hammered at his cheeks. Flying at the speed of light had never felt so good. As Planet Earth shrunk behind him, suddenly, and without warning, a blast knocked him from his path. In seconds he had lost all sensation in his arms and chest. With an icy terror, the paralysis spread to his legs and feet and he plunged into freefall, accelerating until he became nothing more than another fiery comet in the night sky.

Down he hurtled, G-forces contorting his face. No longer could he see Planet Earth in its entirety, no longer could he see America mapped out before his eyes.

If his computer-like brain was right, he was about to land, smack-bang on top of The Statue of Liberty! Desperately, he tried to force life into his useless limbs, but they refused to listen. He had no choice except to brace himself for impact . . .

Mouse fell back onto the beanbag and shook the life back

into his cramped fingers. He had no idea how long he had been drawing, but as he gazed at the wall, he was happy with what he saw. Delighted, in fact.

Now, some people might try and tell you that the painting on the ceiling of the Sistine Chapel in Rome is the most sublime work of art ever created. That it can move a person like no other painting in the world. Well, my friends, let me tell you this: that is complete and utter bobbins. That person obviously hasn't laid eyes on the walls in Mouse's bedroom. These are things of beauty, masterpieces, comic-book adventures to both stun and entertain anyone who looks upon them.

And the best thing about them is that they happened entirely by accident.

Mouse had moved up to the attic just before the triplets were born, and he was happy about it too. He loved the fact that when he pulled up the rickety metal ladder and shut the hatch,

all the racket and hullabaloo downstairs was muffled.

The room was his and his alone, with no grubby little hands pawing at his rare and valuable comics.

He and Dad had decked it out themselves, talking endlessly as they worked.

Who's your favourite superhero, Dad?

Superman, no contest.

Was he even invented back then?

They'd laughed and teased and joked as they carpeted the floor and plastered the walls, undercoating them white, ready for Phase Two. But Phase Two had never happened. Because the triplets arrived five weeks early and then stayed in hospital for another five. And when they finally *did* come home, Dad didn't have the time or energy to stick a paintbrush in his hand.

The only things he ever held in his fist these days were a wand, an animal he'd pulled from his hat, or a pungent nappy bag.

Mouse's walls remained the purest white, like an untouched piece of paper, which after six frustrating months gave him the idea. If Dad didn't have time to decorate his room in rare, limited edition comic book wallpaper, Mouse would just have to do it himself. Which he did, brilliantly.

You have never seen the likes of it.

Metre after metre of the most daring superhero adventures ever created, all painstakingly illustrated by Mouse, and all starring him. He was the hero. No twins, no triplets, just him. This was his escape. All Mouse had to do to become a hero was pick up his pen, and there he was, his alter ego, the Boy Wonder sent from the outer reaches of time and space, the one and only, Mouse the Mighty!

There was no mission too great for this pint-sized hero, no adversary too big. Boys wanted to be him, girls wanted to be *with* him, but Mouse the Mighty had no time for such frivolities. Not when the world was constantly in the clutches of his nemesis, Dr Well 'Ard. Battle after battle filled over two of Mouse's walls: smackdowns in space, underwater duels, even arm-wrestling atop the world's greatest landmarks. There was nowhere in the galaxy that this rivalry wouldn't reach, and every part of it filled Mouse with joy.

Well, sort of. Because this comic strip kind of summed up Mouse's problem. I mean, what good was it, being the world's bravest superhero, or even the world's best drawer of superheroes, if no one knew about it?

For months he'd been trying to tempt Mum or Dad up the rusty loft ladder to show them what he'd been doing. But Dad was always working or kipping on the sofa. And as for Mum – by the time she managed to get the other five into bed, she didn't have the energy to climb the ladder in her tights, never mind the one up to Mouse's room.

Tonight, though, Mouse was so proud of the new cliffhanger on his wall, Mum just HAD to see it. Once she did, Mouse knew she'd be skipping up the ladder every night, desperate to see just what a hero her son really was. With great gusto (for someone with a banged up ankle), he ripped open the loft hatch, kicked the ladder into position and slid, like Batman down the Batpole.

'Mum!' he called, not caring if the triplets or twins were asleep. 'Mum! Come and check this out!'

But as his feet hit the carpet, he knew that his plans had·been scuppered. There, in the doorway to the triplets' bedroom, lay Mum, fast asleep, dribble escaping from the side of her mouth.

What's the problem? I hear you cry. *So she's asleep? Wake her up, Mouse, wake her up!*

It wasn't quite as simple as that, though, because Mum wasn't the only person in the doorway. Across Mum's slumbering body lay five other snoring bundles: Dean, Roger, Bruce, Peter and Clark.

Mouse felt as if he'd been pricked with the world's biggest pin. So deflated was he that he considered joining his brothers. At least that way, when Mum woke, she might notice him. Instead, he did what he did most nights on finding his mum asleep on the landing. He tucked a pillow beneath her head, turned on the radiator nearby and crept back up the ladder to his room. There was a galaxy that needed saving, and it wasn't going to save itself.

Mouse Makes a Splash

Another normal, humdrum day in Seacross. Not that Mouse's supersonic senses (or eyes and ears, as they were commonly known) were ever set on 'Stand-by'. He knew better than that.

Take this afternoon, for instance, a dull wet Tuesday, made duller and wetter by the fact that Mouse's class had swimming lessons at the local sports centre.

Mouse was in the middle of trying to change into his trunks (dancing clumsily while holding a towel around his modesty) when he heard the unmistakable sound of panic echo in his bat-like ears.

Nobody else seemed to notice, which pleased Mouse (maybe he really did have powers after all), so with a final shimmy he dropped the towel, and strutted, still wearing his school shirt with his trunks, into the pool area.

Maybe it was the incredible drawing he'd done last night, but Mouse was brimming with an unusual confidence. There was no doubt in his mind that today was the day when everyone would see him in a new and super light. And, man, was he excited about it.

But there was no Dr Well'Ard waiting for him at the poolside.

This enemy wasn't drawn in pencil. This enemy was *way, way* uglier.

Masher Milner.

Now Masher may have been the most villainous bully-boy in the town of Seacross, but today Mouse couldn't walk away. *What would Iron Man do?* he said to himself, as he started to assess the situation fully. It didn't take him long, because there, being dangled by his ankles over the deep-end of the pool by Masher, was *poor* Danny Christmas.

Danny was poor for a lot of reasons. He was the shortest kid, not only in Mouse's class, but in the whole school, and he wasn't exactly gifted when it came to things other kids deemed important, like sport, or indeed any kind of bodily co-ordination. It didn't help that his dad was a vicar. It wasn't that the other kids mocked him for his pa's religious beliefs. Oh no, it was simpler than that. You see, being a vicar made Danny's dad *Father Christmas*. And, well . . . you have to admit, that's kind of funny . . .

Anyway, Danny . . . ha, ha . . . oh, I'm sorry, it just tickles me. *Father Christmas* . . .

To the delight of his lapdogs, Saliva Shreeve and Bunions Bootle, Masher was clutching the writhing Christmas elf with minimum effort.

'This is how your dad christened me. Now it's your turn . . . ' he said. And with great glee, he dipped Danny into the pool, like a digestive in a milky cup of tea.

Danny re-emerged coughing and spluttering, tears barely masked by the dripping water. It was an action too far for Mouse, who marched straight up to Masher and prodded him in the back. He'd never dared lay a finger on Masher before, but he'd never seen an injustice as clear as this one and today he couldn't stop himself. He might have been bricking it, but he knew from his comics that these were the sorts of moments that defined you, that made the world sit up and notice. In his case, for the first time.

Taking a deep breath, on Mouse went.

'I think that's enough, don't you?' he barked, in his firmest superhero tones.

Masher and his pals didn't see Mouse's interruption as *Superman-esque*. They swatted him away like an irritating bluebottle at a barbecue, before dunking Danny once more.

'I said, leave him ALONE!' Mouse laid his hands on the middle of Masher's back now. But Masher didn't move, not a centimetre. Instead he turned and picked Mouse up effortlessly by his school tie, which in turn made Mouse's shirt ride halfway up his back. Suddenly, Mouse wasn't feeling half as brave.

'Here! What's he got on under his shirt?'

Mouse froze.

Oh no. He'd forgotten all about that. Masher hadn't seen it, had he?

'Look!' The bully laughed and pulled the shirt higher. 'He is, you know, this wally's wearing a *cape*!'

Mouse felt his cheeks flush a brighter red than the material tied around his neck.

He'd had the cape for as long as he could remember. Couldn't recall a time when he didn't wear it proudly, obsessively, under his clothes. As a four year old, he'd screamed when Mum tried to take it off at bedtime. Every night she gave in, returning an hour later to prise it from his neck and wash it while he slept.

Cute, I know, but right now, it wasn't doing him a lot of favours.

Masher, Saliva and Bunions howled with laughter, clawing clumsily at the buttons before pulling Mouse's shirt off and throwing it into the pool.

Mouse's classmates started to gather by the changing rooms, some laughing, others bemused by the sight in front of them. Why was Mouse taking on the three most feared idiots in the whole school? And if he really did fancy himself as a superhero, where was the rest of his costume? Superman never sent his to the dry cleaners, not when he was on duty. He probably had a spare, or seven of them in fact. One for each day of the week, like those pants your mum bought you last Christmas – Monday, Tuesday, Wednesday – you know the ones?

No? Just me?

Well, anyway, Masher wasted no time in seizing on poor Mouse's mistake, marching him along the edge of the pool as Danny Christmas scrabbled to safety.

'I had no idea you lived this amazing double life,' Masher said. 'This is incredible. All these years you've been living in our midst and we had no idea.'

'Put me down. People are watching.' Mouse could feel himself blushing. Why hadn't he remembered about the cape? After all, he wore it on purpose every day, to make himself feel like a hero, even if people didn't see him that way.

'They're watching 'cos they're as impressed as me. And you know what? I reckon they want to see exactly the same thing I do.'

'W-w-what's that?' Mouse asked, not really wanting the answer.

'Well, it's simple, innit?' Masher said, climbing the steps that ran alongside the deep end. 'If you really are a superhero, then me, them, all of us, we want to see you fly!'

Mouse's head stopped spinning enough to realise where he was. Twenty metres above the surface of the pool, on the highest diving board. The place where only the bravest – or the craziest – dared to tread.

'Put me down!' he yelled, throwing punches that were nowhere near hitting their target.

'But I don't need to, do I? 'Cos if I let go . . . you'll just float. That's how it works, isn't it?'

Mouse wanted to scream in frustration. Of course, that's how it *should* work, for a proper superhero. More than anything in the world, he needed it to be the case, but he knew that wishing wasn't going to make it happen.

'You ready then?' Masher said. There was a mixture of cries and laughter from the audience. Mouse saw Jake and Floss banging on the window of Reception, trying to catch the eye of a teacher, an off-duty superhero, or the lifeguard, who should have been paying attention instead of chatting up the receptionist.

Whoever came running, they'd be too late. For Masher had begun a countdown that involved humming the Superman theme tune, and Mouse knew that once he finished . . .

As it happened, Masher didn't even wait that long, preferring the dramatic approach of letting go mid-hum. With a cry that sounded anything but super, Mouse tumbled. No matter how hard he tried to pull himself into a dive position, it was impossible. His cape had betrayed him and was whacking him distractingly about the face. With a sickening thud, Mouse belly-flopped into the pool. The water responded angrily, jumping out and soaking everyone watching, including the teachers as they arrived agonizingly late.

Mouse surfaced, stomach throbbing. He took one look at the angry, sodden faces poolside and knew he wasn't going to be popular. This was no hero's reception, not by a long shot.

6

Missing in Action

A sore stomach, bruised pride and a damp cape made for a slow and painful walk home. It had been a loooooooooong day.

The mickey-taking had been inevitable, though it felt a bit much when the lifeguard on duty had started humming the theme to Superman as he pulled Mouse from the pool.

'Did you not realise you still had the cape on?' Jake asked, as they reached Storey Street, where he, Mouse and Floss lived.

Mouse stared at his best pal in disbelief. ''Course I did. First thing I did when I woke up this morning was think, "Oooh, I must remember to humiliate myself in front of everyone

I know." What do you think?'

'Don't be like that,' Jake said, putting his arm around Mouse. 'It's just . . . well . . . it's unusual, isn't it? You know, to wear a cape when you're not . . . '

'Not what?'

'Well . . . when you're not *actually* a superhero.'

Another bolt of pain jolted through Mouse's body, stronger than anything he was already feeling. He couldn't help being fascinated by caped crusaders. Not when he was similar to so many of them. Ignored, mocked, anonymous. At least until they had their moment to shine, to show the world how amazing they really were. When was *his* moment coming?! Even if he didn't ever develop any proper powers, he still believed there was something special about him, that in some way he could make a difference. He tried to think of a way to explain this without sounding like a wally, but couldn't.

He said goodbye to his friends, and padded through his front door. Except today he wasn't to be invisible among the usual chaos. Today Mouse was going to going to make more noise than the lot of them. Today he was going to stand in the hall and wail and cry and stamp his feet.

If that was what it took to make Mum realise he needed her

time as much as his brothers did, then so be it.

Mouse hung his cape on the radiator to dry, then stood and filled his lungs with air. But before he began to wail, he noticed a blur above him at the top of the stairs. Within seconds, the blur was halfway down the banister, and a heartbeat later, it had knocked him flat on his bum.

'Dean?' Mouse shouted, climbing to his feet and putting his brother on the floor. 'That's dangerous! What were you thinking? Where's Mum?'

No sooner had he finished those words than another blur sped towards him. You see, whatever Dean did, Roger wasn't to be outdone, and Mouse found himself on the floor again, the other twin giggling on top of him.

'What is wrong with you two?' It was bad enough being ganged up on at school, without been terrorised by a couple of miniature bullies at home too.

The twins were always up to no good, like any three year olds, but it wasn't like Mum to let them anywhere near the stairs unsupervised. Where was she?

Dean and Roger were so high from their rollercoaster ride that Mouse couldn't get any sense out of them, so he went in search of Mum himself.

The lounge was silent. There was no sign of Dad's many work pets. He obviously wasn't back from trying to entertain today's reluctant crowd.

Mouse walked towards the kitchen, picking up muffled signs of life getting louder as he plodded closer. It wasn't the normal racket. He couldn't hear the triplets wailing or laughing. No, the loudest noise seemed to be coming, unless he was mistaken, from his dear old mum.

'Mum?' he called, pushing the door open. Davina the dove thrashed past him in a bid for freedom, followed by Frederico, Reg, Tamara and Cedric. That's when Mouse knew something was wrong. Mum *never* let the animals run free near the triplets, and she definitely never let the boys crawl inside their cages as they were doing now.

Mouse fought the temptation to close the cage doors, imprisoning the triplets, and focused on Mum, who was slumped

over the dining table.

'Mum?' he asked, gently shaking her shoulder. 'Are you all right? Where's Dad?'

Mum lifted her head reluctantly, make-up smudged so badly she looked like a panda that hadn't slept in months.

'I don't know!' she wailed. 'That's the problem!'

Mouse was confused, and a little bit scared. Mum wasn't a crier, and she wasn't a wailer either, despite the levels of chaos that her six adorable, slightly bonkers children threw at her every day. Right now she didn't even seem bothered that Clark was currently munching on what looked like droppings he'd found in the bottom of Frederico's cage. Something BIG had gone on, and it clearly involved Dad.

'What's going on? Where's Dad?' Mouse asked again and turned to head for the stairs. The last thing he wanted to do was hunt for Dad, especially after the day he'd had.

'Don't bother looking for him,' Mum cried. 'You won't find him. They looked everywhere!'

Mouse was baffled. 'Who did?'

'Mrs Finigan, from Number 7. It was her Paddy's birthday party Dad was playing at.'

'But it's not as if Dad will have got lost,' Mouse said. 'You can walk there in about thirty seconds!'

Mum steeled herself with a deep breath. Mouse did the same. What was she about to tell him?

'It was the grand finale,' Mum wept. 'You know, the bit where he normally makes the birthday boy or girl disappear?'

Mouse nodded. He'd seen it a gazillion times. There was a secret area at the back of Dad's 'vanishing' box, just big enough for a kid to hide in for a minute or two. It was a showstopper, the highlight of the act.

Mum went on. 'Well, today, Dad didn't ask Paddy to hide in the box, did he? No today, he squeezed inside it himself. Mrs Finigan said he was smiling the whole time. Happiest he's looked in years, she said.'

A sob shook Mum's body before she continued.

'So after dropping the lid on himself, he shouted the magic words, there was a puff of smoke, then – nothing. Silence. The kids thought it was hilarious, thought it was all part of the act. Only when it went on for longer than a minute, they started to get bored. They threw pineapple on sticks at the box until Mrs Finigan opened the lid and found it empty.'

'Empty? What do you mean empty? He must've been hiding in the secret bit.' Mouse was confused, and increasingly nervous.

He didn't like where this was going.

'She looked in there, and that was empty too. Apart from this.'

Mum held up a soggy piece of paper, the ink on it smudged by her tears.

Mouse took it from her and squinted at the words. Although smeared, he could still make out what the note said.

Dear Jo, Mouse, Dean, Roger, Bruce, Peter and Clark,

I'm sorry to do this to you, but I think it's for the best.

You see, I can't do it any more. I'm tired.

So tired I can't think straight.

So tired I can't even pull a rabbit out of a hat in an entertaining fashion. And I'm definitely too tired to saw anyone in half.

The only thing I can do safely, is this – make myself disappear. It's for the best. You've enough to do without a useless, good-for-nothing husband and father too.

I know you'll be cross, and I know you won't understand. But I'm sorry. For everything.

I hope in time you might forgive me.

With love,

Marvin (The Magnificent)

Mouse was SO confused. His emotions raged. How could Dad do this to them? He'd known Dad was fed up and tired, but he hadn't known it was this bad. Should he, Mouse, have done more to help? Told him how great his act was, or let him sleep longer when he needed a nap? Mouse read the letter again. And again. But every time the words said the same thing. Dad was gone. And he didn't say when he'd be back.

'Mrs Finigan was furious,' Mum said. 'Stood on the doorstep, in front of the whole street and demanded her money back. My purse was empty 'cos I'd just paid the window cleaner – I had to take the cash from Clark's moneybox. Can you imagine the shame?' She sobbed again on Mouse's shoulder. Mouse saw the remains of Dad's 'vanishing' box behind her, smashed into a gazillion pieces.

'Did Mrs Finigan do that? Wow, she really was cross.'

Mum looked momentarily sheepish. 'No, that was me. I had to make doubly sure Dad really wasn't hiding in it. You know what he's like. He can sleep anywhere . . . ' and with that came more tears.

Mouse hugged her and stood tall. 'It'll be all right, Mum. I promise it will. All those things Dad used to do, like cleaning or babysitting while you work? Well, I can do them. I'll get a job. A paper round! No problem.'

He looked towards the triplets, wondering how long it would take him to wrestle them into their pyjamas. He wanted to help, to be the man about the place if his dad wouldn't. But Mouse was scared too. He might have been a superhero in waiting, but he wasn't an adult. Nor did he have any desire to be. Not that it felt like he had any choice right now.

Clark was still in the rabbit cage. He looked sweetly at Mouse. Mouse smiled back. Maybe this wouldn't be so bad. Then Clark vomited, a wave of bunny-dropping puke that trickled towards Mouse's feet.

Things were about to get complicated.

More Than a Mere Mortal

Every superhero has an origins story. That moment in time which turns them from an Ordinary Joe into an Extraordinary one.

Mouse's mum, Jo, had never really been ordinary in the first place, not in Mouse's eyes. She was Head Chef, Chief Cleaner, Chief Executive of EVERYTHING that went on in their house, but the day his dad disappeared, it became Mum's equivalent of being bitten by a radioactive spider. At that moment, she had no choice but to upgrade from mere mortal to *superhuman*.

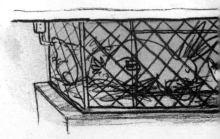

When Mouse got up the following morning, he wondered what sort of state he was going to find Mum in. He'd tried to help her tidy the kitchen before going to bed, but she wasn't having

any of it. She'd packed him off to his room with a hug. So Mouse

was surprised, when he arrived downstairs, carrying a box of

tissues from the bathroom, to find a scene of perfect domestic

bliss. Well, by their standards at least.

The twins were noisily devouring round after round of toast,

the triplets happily chewing on a mixture of fists and toys. Dad's

work zoo had been stored in their various enclosures beneath the

table, and the debris from the vanishing box had, well, vanished.

Mum was standing at the sink, washing up.

She turned as he entered, her panda eyes

replaced by a pair of

glistening diamonds,

shining at the sight of her eldest boy.

'Morning, sweetheart,' she said. 'There's porridge on the table for you, with honey. Oh, and I cleaned your school shoes. They were in a right old state.'

Mouse's mouth fell open. Firstly, over the breakfast. Honeyed porridge was his favourite, but usually he got it once a year on his birthday (if he was lucky), as Mum was way too busy to make it. A normal breakfast consisted of Mouse rummaging through the cupboards for the last of the cornflakes or choco pops. On the really grim days, he had to pour whatever his brothers had left into his own bowl. Hardly the breakfast of champions, let alone superheroes.

Secondly, let's talk about the shoes. Shoes NEVER got cleaned in their household. It was deemed a successful day if everyone left the house with clean faces, but things you put on your feet? Forget about it.

Mouse stared at his polished black loafers, and tried not to fall over them as he followed his nose towards the porridge.

Mum carried on buzzing around while Mouse ate his breakfast, effortlessly mopping up the debris around him, giving the twins a drink each and putting shoes on their feet.

What was going on? Had yesterday's events even happened?

Maybe it had all been a bad dream and he'd find Dad in his default position, asleep on the settee?

Mouse's pulse sped. That would be amazing, because then his brain wouldn't have to cope with being angry, sad and scared all at once. He got up and sprinted to the living room, ready to help Dad in any way he could, to make sure he'd never even dream of leaving them. But the only snoring in there was coming from one of Dad's cages. Mouse's shoulders sagged as he walked back to his porridge, which suddenly didn't taste so sweet.

'Did Dad call last night?' he asked Mum, who was wiping Peter's nose as she whipped away a heavy nappy. He really hoped he had called. To make sure they were all OK. Surely it was the least he could do?

'He didn't love, no.'

'Did you ring him?'

'By the time I got the dishwasher loaded, unloaded and put away, I could barely keep my eyes open.'

'Maybe I should try him. See if he answers.'

'Not now, Mouse, eh?' She tried to look cheerful. 'Tonight maybe. Or tomorrow.'

Mouse let the subject drop, partly because he didn't know what to say. It was weird – Mum *seemed* to be all right now.

I mean, she'd cleaned his shoes for heaven's sake! Surely he should just be grateful? But it didn't feel right somehow. He decided to stop worrying and help, fastening the triplets into their super-wide pram, and making the twins stand on the buggy boards behind them.

Mum, in the meantime, was pulling on her lollipop lady uniform of a high visibility coat and peaked hat, while clamping a two-metre long lollipop stick between her knees. Even when getting dressed, she was an awesome multi-tasker.

'Shouldn't you have the day off?' asked Mouse. 'I'm sure school would understand.'

'And who'd get all you lot across the road safely? Besides, it gets me out of the house. I'd go mad sitting here all day.'

Just then, Jake and Floss arrived at the door.

'Oh good,' said Mum, clearly relieved at the interruption. 'Off you go, Mouse. And don't be worrying about me. We'll be fine. Long as we look after each other.'

Mouse didn't believe Mum was really OK. Not a jot. He could see her smile was sketched onto her face in faint pencil. And he didn't have a clue how to go about colouring it in.

Mouse traipsed up Storey Street towards school with his pals, who had noticed immediately that all was not well.

'I don't want to talk about it,' he said.

'What's *it?*' asked Jake.

'The thing I don't want to talk about.'

'Yeah, we get that bit, but come on. We want to help,' said Floss.

Mouse umm-ed and ahh-ed, but by the time they reached the school gates, he had told them the whole sad story.

'Where do you think your dad might be then?' Floss asked finally.

'If I knew that, do you think I'd be here? I'd be banging on his door to wake him up. I'd drag him home by his bow tie.' He meant it too, could feel a surge of anger at Dad for doing this to them.

'We could help you look for him,' Jake offered. 'I mean, Seacross isn't that big, and although your dad's a decent magician, he can't disappear for ever.'

'Hang on,' interrupted Floss. 'Don't you remember what happened last time we went looking for a missing dad? We ended up trapped in that derelict building and almost got crushed to death!'

The boys shivered at the recollection, though I have to say it is actually a very entertaining and funny story, and one that is definitely worth buying from any good bookshop.

Matters weren't helped when they reached the school gates and Mouse spotted Masher and pals loitering, presumably waiting to torment him again. Brilliant. With everything going on at home, he'd forgotten about what had happened yesterday. How was he going to cope with this as well?

'Look,' Bunions said, with a guffaw. 'It's Splatman. The greatest belly-flopping hero this world has ever seen.' And with that Masher and Saliva hoisted Mouse into the air and flew him round the playground, despite Floss and Jake's protests, and to the other kids' hilarity.

Mouse felt every bit of 'superness' drain out of him. He should've fought back.

But he already had too much to worry about, like Mum. He had to be strong for her and for his brothers. Not get into pointless fights at school.

He remembered what she'd said – that they needed to look after each other, like Batman looked after Robin. That was it. They would become their very own band of superheroes, like The Avengers, except on a much lower budget. He loved The Avengers. They were some of his favourite comic book heroes. The way they stood together. How, united, no one could defeat them. The thought cheered Mouse as he walked back to the crossing to keep an eye on his brothers as Mum worked. It gave him the strength to get through what was a very testing day. It would have cheered him even more, if he'd known what was going to happen next . . .

CCCCRRRRRREEAAAK, CRAAAAACCCKKK...

It took about a week, (despite both Mum's and Mouse's best intentions) for the cracks to begin to show. Let's be fair, it wasn't a massive surprise. I mean, the sum was a simple one, even for a thicko like me:

Six kids ÷ by one parent = UTTER CHAOS!

The house looked as if it belonged to a pig with a broken vacuum cleaner, while cobwebs had appeared that were so huge it looked like Spiderman had moved in.

Mum was doing her best, but after her impressive start, she just couldn't get on top of everything. Not when she was so dog tired.

Mouse's shoes hadn't been cleaned since the day after Dad left. And it wasn't just his shoes that felt neglected. Mouse felt it too. It was weird without Dad there. He kept hoping to hear his keys turning in the door, or find him practising a new trick in the living room. He missed him and hated him in equal measure. And it wasn't easy feeling that way.

Despite Mum's superhero efforts, there was never quite enough food in the cupboards or clean spoons in the cutlery drawer. The washing basket had erupted and was spilling down the stairs, and even though he'd asked for help with his homework every night for a week, the pages of Mouse's exercise book remained blank. It made him realise that maybe Dad hadn't just slept *all* the time.

Everyone was feeling uptight. Something had to give, and eventually it did . . .

Things always got super-tense in the lead-up to leaving the house for school. Being lollipop lady was a great responsibility, and Mum hated the thought of her lateness leaving even one child to brave the road alone. She liked to be on her crossing for 8.15am, which meant leaving the house at 8.07am precisely.

OK, you might be thinking, what's stressful about that? Well, first, Mum had to wash, dress, feed, and change the nappies of five little people, instead of leaving the twins and triplets behind with Dad. She also had to force ten wriggling arms into five coats, and ten kicking feet into five pairs of shoes.

It might still not sound like much, but when you're already cream-crackered from doing it by yourself for the previous week let me tell you, it's like trying to transport a sandcastle in a sieve.

Today was proving even more impossible than usual. Dean had just regurgitated his breakfast, while Clark and Bruce had managed to fill their nappies with nuclear waste just seconds after Mum had strapped them into their prams.

'You are kidding me?!' she wailed as she pulled them back out again. 'Mouse, love, have you got everything for school? What day is it?'

'Tuesday.'

'Then where's your swimming kit? Tuesday is swimming day.'

Mouse couldn't believe she'd remembered, especially when he'd done his best to forget. After a week of harassment following that incident, he couldn't face it again.

'Can't I miss it today, Mum?'

Mum didn't look up as she whipped away two nappies simultaneously. 'Are you ill?'

'No.'

'Or lazy?'

'You know I'm not.'

'Then you're going swimming.'

'But I don't want to, Mum.'

She broke away from the nappies, grimacing from the whiff of two toxic bottoms.

'Do I look like I want to do *this*?' she said.

'Well, no …'

'But I'm doing it anyway, aren't I?'

Mouse knew where this was going. 'Yes,' he said reluctantly.

'So go and get your swimming kit. And before you even say it, your towel's in the airing cupboard and your goggles and trunks are in your pants drawer.'

Mouse marched upstairs, slamming his feet in frustration on every step. He was still sulking when he came downstairs with his kit in his hand to find Mum continuing to wrestle with nappies, but with a lot less patience.

For some reason though, instead of taking this as an opportunity to help Mum and get back into her good books, something in Mouse's head short-circuited, and he acted like the biggest baby in the house.

'Where's my bag gone?' he yelled.

'I don't know. Wherever you left it,' said Mum.

'I left it here.'

'You can't have done.'

'Well, I can't go swimming if I haven't got a bag, can I? And if you haven't got the time to even help me look, that's it. Game over.'

He threw his kit down next to her.

Quick as a flash, Mum was on her feet, steam threatening to fizz from her ears.

'Michael Mouse!!' she shouted. 'Don't you think I've enough tantrums from these five, without YOU acting like a toddler as well?'

'I don't care about them. For once, I want you to listen to ME. I don't want to go swimming today. I don't! And not you or anybody else is going to make me.'

Why couldn't she understand that he just couldn't face it? Not with Masher lurking in the shadows. Not when he was still so confused and upset about Dad disappearing.

'Oh,' Mum roared back. 'Well, that, my boy, is where you are wrong!' And with a flourish, she picked up the towel from the floor and threw it around his neck, tying it with a clumsy bow.

Never before had Mouse complained about wearing any kind of cape, but this was different. If Masher and friends caught sight of him, he'd never hear the end of it, especially as the towel was

covered in starfishes and seashells!
He tried to wrestle it from
his neck, but the knot
refused to budge. As
he struggled, Mum
moved onto Stage
Two, and snapped his
goggles on top of
his head.

'Get this towel off me!' Mouse
shouted. 'And these too!'
Mum had pulled the elastic
on the goggles so tight
that oxygen was struggling
to reach his brain.

'I won't! You can go to school wearing them!' she yelled.
'And I'm warning you now, Mouse. One more complaint and
you'll be wearing these trunks ON TOP OF YOUR TROUSERS
too!' She rammed them into his coat
pocket.

Mouse felt all the fight
drop out of him. He could tell

from the expression on Mum's face that she wasn't joking.

Why had he gone and lost his temper? He wouldn't have done it if Dad hadn't legged it. It was Dad he should be shouting at, not Mum. But how could you shout at someone when you had no idea where they were? Oh dear. He had one parent left, and she was livid with him.

What a hole he'd dug himself. Not only was it fifty metres deep, it appeared to have scorpions scurrying around at the bottom, and barbed wire stretched across the top. It would take a superhero of epic proportions to fight his way out of this pit of peril, not one dressed as a complete plonker. When Masher saw him, this was only going to end one way. With pain and humiliation.

But maybe, just maybe, it wouldn't *all* be bad.

Radioactive Wasters

The sniggering started as soon as Mouse hit Storey Street.

Kids, parents, even his best pals, couldn't help seeing a funny side that Mouse refused to acknowledge. He knew that superheroes' alter egos were often teased, but he was sure even Clark Kent had never taken this amount of stick.

It really kicked off once he reached the school crossing. With no Dad to look after his brothers, Mouse had been forced to take on babysitting duties until the bell rang.

This usually proved easy enough with the triplets, who were strapped in their buggy side by side – their loyalty could be bought with supplies of tasteless cardboard rice cakes. But the twins were a different matter. They were neither tied in, nor easily bribed. Today, it was as if they could sense the tension in the air and decided to make it worse. Within seconds, they'd jumped off the buggy boards and were dashing in different directions, giggling like a couple of maniacs.

This left Mouse with no option but to leave the triplets on the pavement, and hunt Dean and Roger down like a sheepdog, albeit a sheepdog wearing an aquatic themed towel and goggles ensemble. Well, you can imagine the hilarity that brought about, can't you? The sight of Mouse's lilac towel billowing out behind him as he ran had Masher and his friends in pieces, inventing new identities for him like 'The Sea WEED'. Mouse tried to ignore them, but when his trunks made a dash for freedom from his pocket, the bullies surrounded him.

'Hang on!' Masher said, spotting Mum was out of earshot. 'Mummy's little soldier isn't properly dressed for battle!'

And with one all-too-easy motion, he tugged the trunks over Mouse's shoes and trousers, snapping the elastic into place and winding our hero in the process.

'There. Perfect. There's no three year old you can't defeat now.'

Mouse couldn't think how to respond. He was too embarrassed.

His trunks might have been a vibrant red, a colour befitting the majestic Superman, but they were also littered with fabric swimming badges that Mum had sewn on. Mouse had read a LOT of comics in his time, and he'd NEVER seen any of his heroes' costumes bragging about their ability to swim doggy paddle for twenty-five metres.

But what Mouse didn't realise was that his fortunes were about to change – big time. Everyone knows that truly magnificent crime fighters are borne out of terrible, mind-boggingly detestable scenarios. Matt Murdock didn't become Daredevil until he was hit by an articulated lorry carrying gallons of radioactive waste, and I can't imagine as that first barrel hit him flush in the face he thought, *Brilliant! Finally I get to be a Superhero!*

What probably went through his mind was

ARRRGGGGHHHHH . . . then *DUCK!* . . . then, too late! . . .
then, *OUCH!*

Well, Mouse was going through a (slightly) less painful version of that radioactive waste moment right now, because what he didn't know was that three miles away, in Seacross town centre, two figures on high-powered motorbikes were racing away from a shop . . .

These two people weren't racing away because they'd just bought the new book by their favourite author and wanted to get home to read it. They weren't even racing away because they'd just purchased a basket of warm croissants from the bakers' shop (oh, yum yum yum). No, no, no. They were in a hurry because they'd just run out of *Bling King* Jewellers, having stolen every ring, necklace, bracelet and gem in the place.

The heist had run like clockwork. Security was non-existent, resistance from the jeweller nothing more than a 'Please, no, it's nearly Christmas'. They hadn't even needed to point their guns in his direction. And when I say guns, I actually mean two ripe bananas camouflaged by a pair of socks covered in gun motifs.

Now, on their bikes and giggling to each other via intercom

at just how easy it had all been, brother and sister team Ernie and Esther D'astardly, were making for the outskirts of Seacross, where they would dump the getaway vehicles, pick up their passports and head for a life of sun, sea and toasted sandwiches in Rio de Janeiro.

'How much do you think we got away with?' Esther asked Ernie.

'Millions!'

'That all?' Esther was ambitious.

'Wazillions then,' answered Ernest, who'd never been good at maths, but was very good as inventing new numbers. He wobbled on his bike as he laughed heartily.

'Be careful, will you, you fool!' Esther snapped. 'You should've let me carry some of the booty. What'd happen if you got caught? I'd be left with nothing.'

This was something that had crossed Ernie's mind lots of times. But there was something about his sister that he'd never trusted. She'd always nicked his toys as kids, so no way he was going to trust her with the trinkets they'd just so lovingly lifted. He'd made sure he was the one carrying those.

'We're not going to get caught. Look around you. There's not a police car in sight, and no sirens either. So unless someone has suddenly made superheroes real, we're home and dry,' said Ernie.

With a D'astardly laugh, he indicated right. There was a shortcut coming up, down a quiet, crummy residential road. As soon as they reached the end of Storey Street, there would be nothing but the open road between them and a life of luxury.

The Accidental Superheroes

Three minutes before the morning school bell was rush hour for Mouse's mum, as frantic parents pulled, pushed and cajoled their adorable brats – I mean, children – into the hands of the brave and foolish saviours we call teachers.

Mum's senses were on overdrive as always, though she expected no trouble. Storey Street was hardly a motorway. She was so focused on her job she didn't realise danger was closer than she could ever have imagined.

On the pavement behind her, Mouse was surrounded by a huge scrum of kids, laughing and jeering as he tried to pull the trunks from over his trousers.

'Get off, will you?' he yelled, ashamed he couldn't think of a tougher response. Not for the first time he wished he could fire lasers from his eyes or webs from his wrists. But right now he didn't think he could even blow a raspberry without bursting into tears. Masher had helpfully tied the drawstring on his trunks into a fearsome triple knot, and every time Mouse pulled and twisted, the elastic drew tighter, cutting painfully into his waist. Why was this happening to him? And why today?

With Mouse distracted there was no one keeping an eye on young Dean and Bruce, who soon got bored of watching their brother being tormented and spotted Mum on the far side of the road. Giggling, they started to cross, not noticing the two black motorcycles speeding towards them. Mum, facing the opposite direction, had just finished her last crossing and laid her lollipop stick over her shoulder contentedly.

Suddenly, Miss Maybury (Mouse's teacher) yelled from the gates in a voice loud enough to wake a hibernating bear.

'JOANNA! BEHIND YOU! THE TWINS!'

Quick as a flash, Mum span on her heels, lollipop stick whirling with her. As she turned, the stick flew accidentally from her hands and whooshed across the street, slamming straight into the engine of one of the motorcycles as it whizzed over the crossing.

There was a collective gasp from the crowd, followed by another as the bike swerved and bucked like an unbroken stallion. With one final lurch, the rider was thrown sky high, his rucksack flying open in the process.

Then, something weird happened. It seemed to suddenly and inexplicably start to rain, which Mouse thought was odd because it was a cold and crisp December day. His eyes broke away from his tormentors and flew heavenwards to see a storm of the most expensive raindrops in history fall from the sky. These droplets weren't water – they seemed to be made of gold and silver. They were glinting like diamonds, sapphires and rubies.

Soon, a thousand pieces of jewellery were pinging off the tarmac, and every parent, teacher and student was dashing into the road, falling to their knees and cramming trinkets into their gaping pockets. It was as if Christmas had come early and everyone was getting the same thing. Rich!

The only people not completely besotted by these gifts were Mouse and his mum, who were focused on the twins, still standing in the middle of the road.

From opposite sides of the street they dashed forward, ignoring the falling rings and bracelets, each of them grabbing a twin's hand. With a mighty tug, they whipped them to safety, not a second too soon, as a second black motorbike sped between them, exactly where the boys had been standing.

Thirty metres ahead of the crossing, the second motorbike skidded to a halt. Esther D'astardly couldn't believe what she was seeing. She lifted her visor, but the view remained the same.

'Ernie!' she yelled into her intercom, as she stared at her brother and his bike, both of which had come to rest among a large pile of stinking black bin bags on the roadside. 'Ernest! For goodness' sake, what have you done?'

A groan echoed in her ear. It could've been her own brain voicing its disgust at their plan falling to pieces, but it was more likely to be her idiotic brother.

'Come and help me, will you?' Ernie said. 'This rubbish stinks and I think I've a haddock bone wedged down my trousers.'

Esther's lips curled up in disgust. No way was she getting involved in that little drama. Besides, her mind was focused on one huge final diamond that had fallen without anyone else spotting it.

It was a beast of a gem, the biggest they'd lifted by far, and one that she'd earmarked for herself, set into a ginormous ring or necklace. So when she'd seen it again, she'd started to salivate.

Down it had spun, light reflecting cosmically through it, until it landed, not on the street with all the others, but on the top of a child's buggy. Not your normal pram, this was a beast of a model that housed three whimpering grubby-faced little urchins. The mere sight of them made Esther want to bring up her breakfast.

Eyes widening, she'd watched as the diamond bounced upon the pram's canopy, and rolled precariously towards the edge.

'NOOOOOOO!' she'd cried. If it hit the pavement it would surely crack and its beauty (and value) would be lost forever, but she knew, even on her bike, she couldn't catch it in time. She had to merely watch it bounce and roll until it fell, almost in slow motion . . . straight into a large canvas bag that seemed to be brimming with nappies and other ridiculous baby-detritus.

At the moment it was saved she'd wanted to leap for joy. But that simply wasn't possible with a 750cc motorbike underneath her, so she revved her engine instead. It would take her a few seconds to whizz back there, pluck the gem from the bag and speed away. As she moved forwards, her senses were filled with new and worrying signs: flashing blue lights and whining police sirens.

No! This couldn't be happening. Not now. Not when she was so close to salvaging *something* from her brother's almighty mess.

The police's arrival left her with three options:

1. Save her useless good-for-nothing brother so they could escape together.

No. The dipstick deserved to get caught after being foiled by a two-metre lollipop stick.

2. Go back for the diamond in the teeny-tiny hope that she wouldn't get caught in the process.

Hhhhhhhmmm, tempting, but she really didn't like the prospect of prison food.

3. Beat a hasty retreat and concoct a cunning, sinister and evil plan that would see her and the gem safely reunited.

She smiled. It was an evil smile. The sort of smile a fox reserves for when it's feeling particularly sly. She took one last look at the pram, fixed its image in her criminal mastermind of a brain, and sped away in the opposite direction, just as her brother was having handcuffs slapped on him.

She'd be back. And she wouldn't leave without that gem.

Heaven help the person who owned that buggy.

With Great Power...

Storey Street had never seen the likes of it.

Well, actually, that's not quite true. Bonkers stuff seemed to go on there pretty much every day, but this was straight-from-the-cinema blockbuster action.

Within three minutes and twenty-six seconds, the road outside Mouse's school was awash with police cars and riot vans. There were so many blue lights flashing that Vinny Coupland, the DJ who lived at Number 81, turned his stereo up full blast and tried to start an impromptu disco.

Not that the police were in the mood for dancing – they were busy instructing the residents to give up the trinkets that were hanging from their ears, necks or fingers. Nobody really minded, though – five minutes of feeling like a famous movie star was better than nothing. Now they were too interested in watching the mysterious man from the black motorbike being led away by the law.

'Oooooh,' said Elsie Morgan, who lived at Number 73. 'I'm sure I've seen him before – on Crimewatch. Something Dastardly . . . Him and his sister tried to steal an island off the coast of America. Or something like that.'

Folk around her shook their heads in disbelief, gazing as Ernie struggled his way towards the patrol car. He kept looking around, as if he expected to be saved at any second, but when no one showed up, he simply wailed as a burly officer bundled him onto the back seat.

Up at the school gates there was a different kind of commotion. More vans screeched to a halt, but there were no flashing lights, only signs on the side that read 'SEACROSS AT SIX'. The press had arrived and they wanted the scoop.

It didn't take long for everyone to point them in the same direction, straight towards Mouse's mum.

'It's Jo you need to speak to. She foiled the robbery . . . '

'I saw it with my own eyes.'

'All she needed was a lollipop stick and a shed load of bravery.'

Mouse looked on with wonder as a furry microphone was shoved under Mum's nose while she cuddled Roger and Dean.

'Mrs Mouse! Mrs Mouse! Your neighbours tell us you're

responsible for the arrest of one of this country's most prolific armed robbers. Is it true?'

Mouse strained to hear Mum over the wails of the triplets from their buggy. Seeing their distress, Mum tried to scoot past the interviewer to calm them, but the reporter wasn't going to let her move until he had his exclusive.

'Mrs Mouse, did you stop this evil thug from escaping with nearly a million pounds in jewellery?'

Mouse gasped.

What??

How much???

Without hesitation he pushed the triplets closer.

Mum was just as perplexed. 'Who, me? I had no idea who he was or what he was doing. All I cared about was getting my kids out of the road safely.'

The reporter, the dashing Kyle Ramsbottom from *Seacross at Six*, chuckled as Mum bent down to greet Mouse and the triplets, who had forced their way through the crowd. 'Ah, you're one of those reluctant heroes, are you? The modest kind? I've a dozen witnesses who say you wielded that lollipop stick like a martial arts expert and with one vicious throw, you speared D'astardly clean off his chariot.'

Mum chuckled, her cheeks flushing. 'Speared? The silly thing just flew out of my hand as I turned around.'

But just like the reporter, Mouse wasn't settling for any of this modesty malarkey. Even from a distance he'd seen that what Mum had done was amazing. So brave, so fearless – exactly what he would have done in the same position. Mouse felt excitement prickle all over his body. Of course! It all made sense now. This must be where he got his superhero ambitions from. His mum! He'd never loved her more, or felt any prouder, and there was no way he was going to let her avoid her moment in the spotlight.

'Don't you listen to my mum,' he said, smiling. 'Modesty is her middle name. Well, that and Dorothy. She's been secretly training for this moment for years. You don't become a dead-shot with this kind of killing machine without putting in oodles of practice.'

This was more like it. It gave Kyle Ramsbottom something to run with. 'So you're saying your mum knew an incident like this was going to happen.'

'I'm not saying she can see the future,' Mouse was really hitting his stride now. It took all of his concentration not to slip into a dramatic American accent like they did in the movies. 'But when you live in a town as big and as bad as ours . . . ' A number of the crowd listening in looked a bit baffled at this. Was the kid talking about *their* town? 'You have to prepare for every eventuality.'

'From the way you're talking, young man, it seems you're saying your mum here is some kind of . . . superhero,' said Kyle Ramsbottom.

Mouse felt a wave of excitement dance up and down his spine.

'Maybe I am,' he said. 'Maybe that's exactly what I'm saying.'

'Mouse!' interrupted Mum. 'Don't be silly.'

'No it's fine, Mum.' Mouse wasn't backing down. He liked how it made him feel. He was powerful by association! 'You can't hide it any longer. People need to know just how SUPER you really are!'

'So tell me,' said Kyle, shoving the microphone so close to Mouse's top lip that he gave the young man a moustache. 'What superhero name does your mum go by?'

Oh, thought Mouse. *Darn it*. He wasn't ready for that sort of question. It was an important one that needed careful and detailed consideration.

'Well?' Kyle said.

'I'd have thought that was obvious,' said Mouse, stalling for time, staring at Mum and hoping for any kind of inspiration. 'Just look at her.' He gazed at her uniform and like a flash it came to him. 'My mum is . . . Lady Lollipop!'

A gasp went around the crowd. 'Oooooooh.'

Even Mum, though embarrassed, seemed to grow half a
metre in height. In fact, she jumped in and started playing along.

Why wouldn't she? After all, her eldest son was smiling for the first time in a week.

'He's too kind, this son of mine,' she gushed. 'But you ask anyone in the crowd and they'll tell you he's a bit special too. When that second motorbike whizzed through, he jumped onto the road with no thought for his own safety. All he had in his mind was saving his little brother, and that's exactly what he did.'

She pulled Mouse close, despite having the twins in her arms, and Mouse felt tears of pride prickle behind his eyeballs. He had no idea she'd even noticed!

'So it runs in the family then does it? This superhero gene?'

'Too bloomin' right it does,' said Mum, beaming.

'So tell me, young man, if your mum is Lady Lollipop, who does that make you?'

'Me?' boomed Mouse, adopting an accent that was more Seattle than Seacross (though not until he'd checked his underpants, towel and goggles weren't twisted). 'I am Mouse. Mouse the Mighty!'

...Power and Responsibility!

People throw parties for lots of different reasons. Birthdays, weddings, chickenpox . . . don't laugh, it's true, go and ask your mum. Well, go on! OK, are you back? Comfy? Good . . .

Mouse never would have dreamed he'd spend the two hours after a VERY excitable day at school calling friends to invite them to his imaginatively titled 'Come and Watch Me and My Mum on the Six O'Clock News Party'.

And come they did, in their droves. Neighbours, friends from Mouse's class, even the Chief of Police, were in attendance. (Although the Chief might have been better served patrolling the streets.)

Anyway, Chief Waggle was there, sipping, or rather sucking, his cup of tea hesitantly from a baby's bottle. (There were so many people at the party Mum had run out of cups – the only alternative was a bottle belonging to Frederico, and the Chief decided a baby's bottle was preferable to one that had been chewed by a rabbit for the last six months.)

There wasn't a free seat in the lounge, nor a patch of carpet that didn't have someone perched excitedly upon it. Mouse ran around excitedly with bits of food he'd found in the rather starved cupboards. He'd taken care to present it on a silver-effect tray, and there had been a surprising number of takers for diced, over-ripe banana and raisins that he'd discovered stuck to the twins' high chairs. They'd looked fine after a quick rinse in the fish tank.

He really wanted to keep his guests happy – this party had the potential to be a top end to a perfect day. A day where *everyone* had wanted to talk to him. It made a change from the sort of attention he'd been getting lately from Masher and his friends.

Just as the last banana slice was swiped there was an excited yelp from Jake at the front of the room. 'Shush, it's starting, it's starting!'

It was as well. *Seacross at Six*, the only news bulletin worth watching for a good seventeen mile radius. And there, standing on their very own street, was the handsome, debonair news anchor, Kyle Ramsbottom. Someone wolf-whistled.

'A quiet, residential street . . . ' Kyle purred into his microphone.

'You try living on it!!' roared Jake's dad, George.

Mouse threw a cushion which pinged off George's head.
There was no point inviting people round to relive their moment
of glory if nobody was concentrating. And besides, Mouse
was nervous. What if he came across as a bigger nobody than
usual? What if he'd got carried away and talked a right load of
old rubbish that would have people either rolling their eyes or
sniggering at him?

Back on the telly, Kyle was still oozing charm.

'Some might even say a boring street. The kind where nothing
ever happens. A place where people live dull and senseless lives,
waiting for retirement and false teeth . . . ' Cue more cushions
being thrown, this time at the TV.

'But not today!!' Kyle launched into a more excited tone. 'Because today, Hollywood came to Storey Street. Not literally, of course, that would be impossible. What I mean is that today, on this very street, two brave Seacross residents foiled the biggest robbery in our town's history. With no thought for their own safety, and with only the welfare of their huge family in mind, they single-handedly apprehended uber-criminal and seasoned jewel thief, Ernest D'astardly. A second suspect, believed to be D'astardly's sister, Esther, remains at large, and is described as cunning, manipulative and more driven than a fifty year old car.'

A shot of Ernest being led away prompted a chorus of boos to ring in Mouse's ears. It was like being in the middle of his own pantomime, for a second later there were cheers instead, as Kyle interviewed first Mum, then him.

He stared at the screen transfixed, reliving every second, especially that wonderful moment when finally, the world, or Seacross at least, realised that he really was a special kind of hero, with or without any *real* special powers.

And actually, the more he looked at his beach towel, goggles and trunks, the more he saw that actually, it was a look he could pull off. Comfortably. In fact, he was blinkin' smashing it!

'So, Mouse,' Kyle was asking on screen, 'Or do I call you

Mighty? Tell me about your brothers. Because if you're a superhero, and your mum is too, then surely . . .?'

'Oh, yes,' boomed Mouse. 'Though their skills aren't as practised or as slick as ours yet. We call them the Boy Blunders.'

'And what about their pram here?' laughed Kyle, clearly enjoying himself. 'It's big enough to be a tank. Does it double up as your vehicle?'

He didn't think Mouse would have an answer that for that. But he did. He always had answers for questions of a superhero nature.

'Yes, of course.' Mouse smiled, grabbing the buggy and making the canvas bag on the back shake viciously. 'This is the Bratmobile. It does speeds no other buggy in the world is capable of. And it handily has lots of space for storage,' he added, pointing at the bag.

'Looks like your whole world is full of superheroes,' Kyle said. 'So tell me, Mouse, do you think there are more people like you and your mum in Seacross? People who have the same bravery, the same desire to fight injustice?'

Mouse puffed his chest out like a cockerel about to let fly at dawn.

'There definitely are. And never mind Seacross, there are more on this street. Maybe they just don't know it yet.'

'And what would you say to these people?'

Mouse's head had spun slightly at that question. He knew it was a big one. One he had to get *just* right. So he looked around him, at the sea of faces peering back. He'd lived among these people all his life. Gone to the same school, washed their cars for a quid, played pranks on them on Hallowe'en. None of them were famous. None of them probably ever would be either. But they were good people all the same. They were just like him. And imagine the fun they could have if some of them wanted to be heroes just like him.

'I'd tell them to come and join us. That there's no such thing as a normal person. We're all superheroes.'

His mind had thrown up that old Spiderman quote: *With great power, comes great responsibility.*

'Sometimes being normal can make you extraordinary. Sometimes, with no power, comes great responsibility. So I'd tell people like us to stand up, be proud, and come and find us. Imagine what we could do if we are united!' And with amazing dexterity, Mouse had turned the *Bratmobile* 180 degrees and moved it through the crowd, who parted and cheered the Mouse family every step of the way home.

Back in the living room, Mum looked a bit embarrassed by the new wave of applause and affection on display. 'Oh, stop it, you lot. The stick just flew out of my hand. Any of you would've done the same if your kids were stranded in the street.'

'Well, according to your Mouse,' said Malcolm Pulse, Storey Street's resident undertaker, 'we're all wearing capes under our clothes.'

'Not me,' giggled Katerina Curlers, who owned the hair salon *Curl Up and Dye*. 'Though I do have excellent X-ray vision!'

Everyone had a laugh at that one. Not that Mouse cared. He'd said it. He believed it. And why not? It could be true. Stranger things had happened.

Meanwhile, Across Town...

Loads of people watched the News that night. Some laughed at Mouse's words, some thought him brave, one or two reckoned he should be put in a straitjacket, but no one felt angry while watching him. Well, except one person.

Across town, in a subterranean hideaway (a dingy basement, actually, but we're talking about a super-criminal here, so let's keep it dramatic), Esther D'astardly prowled around, seething.

'Look at the little runt,' she *seethed*. I like that word by the way, seethed, the way it hisses between your teeth when you say it again and again. I might use it a lot in this chapter, so get used to it. 'And his mother too. The sight of them makes me *seethe* with anger.'

She wasn't joking either. It had been a shocker of a day. It didn't bother her so much that her brother had been arrested, more that he'd managed to be nicked while in possession of every single jewel that they'd stolen.

Within an hour of all it going south, she'd had a call from their lawyer, Saul McShiftyson, telling her she needed to pay Ernest's bail – all twenty thousand pounds of it. As if she had that sort of money lying around! If she did, she'd have already been on her way to the airport with it crammed into her underwear. Instead she was trapped in this dark, damp basem . . . I mean, subterranean hideaway, seething about the fact that she was broke, all thanks to that geeky kid and his good-for-nothing lollipop-wielding mother.

She watched as the kid pretended to be some Boy Wonder, her eyes widening as the babies' buggy honed into view. It didn't take much to remind her of what she'd seen before she'd sped away, how that last, ultra-valuable diamond had rolled into the bag hanging on the back of it.

She had to get her hands on that bag. Thirty seconds would be all she needed to find the gem, but how would she get close enough without raising suspicion? It would some serious cunning, and time she might not have. The police knew she and Ernie always worked together, and that wimp of a brother of hers could have already given up her secret location in exchange for a shorter stay in prison.

'Think, Esther!' she seethed, turning back to the television. 'Think!'

The boy was still waffling on . . .

'I'd tell them to come and join us. That there's no such thing as a normal person. That we're all superheroes. Sometimes being normal can make you extraordinary. Sometimes, with no power, comes great responsibility. So I'd tell people like us to stand up, be proud, and come and find us. Imagine what we could do if we are united!'

'Oh, you genius,' Esther grinned. 'You idiotic, but wonderful genius.' And she skipped merrily around the room.

That was it! The boy had spoon-fed her the answer. There he stood, thinking his words made him the toughest vigilante in town, when really, all he'd done was gift Esther the front door keys and access to the jewel that would pay for her life of luxury.

Without hesitation she ran to an old biscuit tin she'd hidden beneath a saggy old mattress. Tearing the lid off, she licked her fingers and counted the wad of notes that lay inside. £875. It wasn't a fortune, but it was enough. Just.

All she needed now was a costume designer with super quick fingers and a boffin with a brain just as fast. And fortunately, because she was a D'astardly sort of person, she knew exactly where to find both.

A Bit Like Hansel and Gretel

The residents of Storey Street had been busy overnight. They might have been an eccentric bunch, but they were also big of heart.

As Mouse and his family opened their door for school, they were faced with the most extraordinary sight. Lining the path to the front gate were two rows of three-metre high, papier-mâché lollipop sticks, just like the one Mum carried for work. The only difference was that on each of the colourful lollipop heads was scrawled a different message:

Lady Lollipop ROCKS!!

Bad guys suck, Lollipop Licks 'em!!

Mouse is More than Mighty!

An amazing sight it was, enough to bring a tear to the eye of the steeliest of hearts. It made their house look a bit like the enchanted cottage in *Hansel and Gretel*, except the Mouse family lived there instead of some mad witch who wanted to eat anyone who stepped inside.

Mouse looked up at Mum, wondering if she was feeling as proud as he was.

Mum pushed a rogue piece of dust from the corner of her eye, ignoring the tears that were leaking out of them too.

'People must think we ROCK!' Mouse said. 'I think we did all right yesterday.'

Mum pulled Mouse into her side and squeezed, before straightening the towel that was tied around his neck again.

'We did do well, didn't we?' she said, beaming, before adding. 'The tag for your swimming trunks is hanging out at the back by the way. Spoils the look a bit.'

'Oh, cheers.' Mouse fiddled with the tag and his goggles too, to make sure he was looking as resplendent as the Man of Steel always did.

There'd been no argument about what he was wearing this morning. Swimming had been and gone (with no bullying obviously), and was another week away now, but there was no way in the world he was going to school without his costume on. Are you kidding me? He'd waited his whole life for this moment. He was the centre of attention, the person everyone at school wanted to be. And was he going to be bashful about it? No bloomin' way.

He glided into school. In fact, there were moments of such elation that it felt like he was flying. There were kind words and slaps on the back, he was even made to stand up in assembly while the rest of the school clapped. Some kids even stood to applaud him. Mouse beamed as he saw Masher begrudgingly banging his hands together. It made a difference from trying to bang them against Mouse's face!

Mrs Maybury even let him wear his costume in class all day too. 'This is just for one more day, though, Mouse,' she warned. 'Tomorrow you go back to proving to me just how *super* you are by working hard at your maths!'

People were still talking about their bravery on the way home, and when Mouse and his mum and brothers reached their front gate, they found more huge lollipop sticks, and proper lollies too, wedged into the fence. Mouse pocketed them before his brothers could.

Some imaginative soul had even made matching superhero outfits for the triplets and twins. Masks and capes in various shades of blue – proper authentic they looked too, though Mouse knew there'd be a riot if they tried to squeeze any of the boys into them. Maybe he'd hang them on his wall instead.

Teatime was as manic as ever. There was noise, and mess, and nappies galore, but somehow he and Mum managed to skate through it with greater ease than normal. They'd catch a glimpse of each other, doing random things like washing up, or wiping a bum, and see that they were still basking in the glow of what had happened.

The only time Mouse's mood dipped was when Dad crashed into his thoughts. What would he make of it all? He'd be proud, wouldn't he? It made Mouse wish more than ever that he knew where Dad was, so he could shout, 'OI! See what you're missing out on? Why would you leave when we're capable of *this?!*' Maybe Dad had seen it on the telly? But if he had, why hadn't he rushed home? It was tough to think about and Mouse refused to give up his good mood.

Gifts and cards continued to arrive all afternoon, endless visitors, just dropping in a casserole or pie.

'We realise how busy you must be, coping on your own.'

'If you can be super, so can we. Well, maybe this shepherd's pie can be, anyway . . . '

Mum accepted the food with a smile and a thank you, but Mouse worried that the gifts might bring her down too, and be

a painful reminder that she was on her own with six kids and a zoo full of delinquent animals. He wanted her to feel super for as long as possible.

By 6.30pm, with the twins and triplets bathed, pyjama'd and milk-bottled in front of the fire, Mouse was glad that the stream of visitors seemed finally to have dried up.

BBBBBRRRRRRNNNNNNNGGGG!

The doorbell piped up with its only-too-familiar ring.

Mum pulled herself to her feet. 'I don't want to seem

ungrateful,' she said, sighing, 'but I don't think there's room in the fridge for another stew.'

'Maybe it'll be more lollipops,' Mouse said, following her.

'I hope not. And I know about the ones you sneaked upstairs after school, young man. My super-sight doesn't miss a thing. Not when it comes to sweets.'

Mouse saw Mum paint a smile on her face as she prepared for another kindly neighbour. But as the door swung open, instead of being faced with a steaming dish of delights, Mouse found himself blinded by a piercing light shining right into his eyes. What evil foe were they facing now? Aliens? Bounty hunters? Mouse panicked when he realised he didn't have his cape on. Mum had insisted they put it in the wash. After all the excitement, it was starting to smell a bit.

'Can we help you?' he asked, trying to sound brave.

The beam flicked off and Mouse's pupils began to shrink as he saw the light had come from a torch on the visitor's cycling helmet.

'Oh, I'm sorry to bother you,' came a voice. 'It's just . . . I saw you on the news. Both of you. And, er . . . well, it's about what you said. I've come, well, I've come to join you.'

Mum frowned, confused.

Mouse grinned.

So it was true. There were others in Seacross just like them. And the more of them there were, the more powerful they would be!

Pound Shop Avengers...

'Join you?' Mum said blankly.

She never was at her sharpest at the end of the day.

The man nodded like an obedient dog, before removing his bike helmet. 'Absolutely. I was gobsmacked by what you did yesterday. So blinking brave, to stand up to that D'astardly guy. Made me think, so it did. Made me want to make a difference. So here I am. I want to be super, just like you.'

Mum didn't know what to say. Her mouth flapped open and shut like a ventriloquist's doll whose owner has a sore throat.

In stepped Mouse. 'That's brilliant!' he said, shaking the man's hand vigorously. 'Come in! Come in!'

The man did as he was told, though he had to crouch slightly to get his looooong body beneath the door frame. Everything about him appeared to have been stretched. He looked like a very thick piece of uncooked spaghetti and was decked from head to toe in black Lycra, though he shimmered in the light thanks to the high visibility strips that littered his clothes. It had a mesmerising effect, and made it look as if electricity was coursing through every centimetre of his massive frame.

'You're so tall!' said Mouse. 'How big are you?'

'Six foot ten,' the man answered, though he didn't look too happy about it. In fact, he seemed to shrink by about thirty percent in shame as he answered.

'You're amazing!' Mouse went to pat him on the back but could only reach his thigh. Imagine how tough this guy would be in a fight. Bad guys would run a mile when they stood in his shadow. 'What's your name?'

'What's my *real* name? Or my superhero one?'

'Both!' laughed Mouse. He couldn't quite believe that what he'd said had made people want to be just like them.

'I'm Nigel. Nigel Bland. I work down the pencil factory.'

'Oh, really? That sounds like, well, it sounds, er . . . ' Mouse couldn't quite bring himself to say it sounded fun. 'It sounds like, well . . . like a job!?'

'Oh, it is. It's definitely that. I stick the rubbers on the end of pencils. It's repetitive, but it pays the bills. Plus the boss said if I keep applying myself, I'll get a promotion. This time next year,

I could be sharpening pencils instead. I'll have real responsibilities.'

Wow, thought Mouse. *I thought I had a boring alter ego, but this guy is a proper pro. There was no way anyone would guess someone with a job as rubbish as Nigel's could possibly be a crimefighter.*

'And what about your superhero name?'

'Oh, I've been thinking about that all day,' Nigel smiled, 'and I think I've come up with a cracker. From this moment on, I want to be known as *Cyclots*.'

Mouse frowned. 'I don't mean to be rude Nigel, but Cyclops has already been spoken for. By the X-Men. You must have seen the guy? Scott Summers? Wears a visor to stop laser beams shooting out of his eyes?'

'No no no,' interrupted Nigel, 'Not CycloPs. CycloT's. Because, well, it's obvious isn't it?' He pointed at his outfit and helmet. 'I cycle a lot. I don't have a car, you see. Can't afford one on a pencil worker's salary.'

Now a lot of people would have burst out laughing when they heard something as lame as that. But not our Mouse. Because he knew how frustrating it was to have your potential ignored by everyone around you. If Nigel's superhero name related to being an awesome cyclist, Mouse was cool with that.

'Where's your bike now?'

'It's outside. Do you mind if I bring it in? Don't want it to get stolen, not with all the thieves about these days.'

Mum frowned, but Mouse said, 'Of course,' then gawped as Nigel wheeled in the largest bike he had even seen in his life. He'd seen bridges that used less metal, and as for the height of it? A giraffe would've struggled to reach the pedals.

'Whoa,' mouthed Mouse. Suddenly there wasn't much space, the bike's bulk pinning him and Mum to the wall.

'Can I get you a drink?' Mum asked.

'Oh, how lovely. Tea, please, if you wouldn't mind. Herbal preferably. Do you have a nettle and thistle infusion?'

Mouse giggled. He'd be lucky if Mum found a tea bag that hadn't already been dunked into a dozen cups. But he liked old Cyclots. He'd certainly never met anyone like him, that was for sure. And if he wanted to form a band of heroes with Mouse and his mum, then that was fine with him.

Before Mouse could pepper his guest with any more questions there was another ring on the doorbell. Cyclots tried to squeeze further down the hall but got tangled in his bike frame and squashed both Mum and Mouse against the coat hooks. Mouse, being the smallest, managed to wriggle free and open the door.

'DAN!' boomed a voice so loud that it scrambled Mouse's brain.

'Er, no. Mouse,' he answered.

'DAN!' yelled the man again.

'Sorry, I'm confused. Either you've got the wrong house, or my name has changed and nobody has told me . . . ' Could this day get any weirder? Mouse thought.

'No.' The man beamed, his smile as wide as his voice was loud. *'I'm* Dan. I saw you on the goggle box. Amazed I was, couldn't take my eyes off it. Thought to myself, these are MY sort of people. So here I am!'

'Are you telling me you're a superhero too?' Mouse's heart thudded in excitement. He couldn't believe it. This guy was normal, just like him, dressed in jeans and a two-tone jumper, black with murky white shoulders. No sign of a cape or mask. But he was here anyway, because of what Mouse had said.

'YES. I suppose I am special. I have a gift anyway. Didn't realise it until I saw what you'd done. Always thought it was more of a curse than a blessing. Now I'm not so sure,' said Dan.

'You'd better come in then,' Mouse said, grinning. 'Mum's putting the kettle on.'

'SMASHING! Tea, milky, four sugars, please. Tablespoons, not teaspoons.'

Five minutes later, once Mum had brewed the tea, the foursome, along with the triplets and twins sat in the living room.

'So,' Mouse said to Dan excitedly. 'Tell us about this gift of yours.'

'Well,' said Dan. 'I've lived with it since I was twelve. For years I thought it made me a freak, but when I saw you and your mum, I decided I was looking at it all wrong!'

Mouse was really excited now. A freak? Was Dan the sort of character he'd read about in the X-Men? A real life bonafide mutant? How cool was that? If he was, imagine the sort of revenge they could exact on Masher and his gang!

'What is it?' he asked. 'Can you read minds? Or control the weather? Oooh, oooh, have you got Adamantium claws like Wolverine?'

'No, nothing of the sort. It's crazier, it's this . . . ' And with that, Dan began to shake his head, immediately causing a strange, otherworldly fog to rise.

Within seconds, Dan's wiry black hair had disappeared, replaced by a thick white cloud, which seemed to be filling the entire room.

Mouse's gob was smacked. He'd never seen anything like it. It was like being caught in the middle of a sudden and threatening snowstorm.

Mum was less than impressed. 'Oh my goodness,' she wailed. 'Is that . . ?'

'It is,' answered Dan from inside the cloud. 'Handy really, because it makes for the perfect superhero name, doesn't it? The name's Druff, Dan-Druff!'

Mouse burst out laughing and he wasn't the only one. The triplets, who'd been showing signs of tiredness, were captivated by the flakes of dead skin floating down around them. The twins were even MORE excited – Dean tried to catch them on his tongue, Roger laid on his back and tried to make a snow angel.

Mum looked horrified at the prospect of either. 'How do you

do that?!' she yelled.

'I don't know,' answered Dan. 'I wash my hair every day, so it's not dirty. It's got to the point where I've stopped saying no to anything, because every time I shake my head . . . '

'Well, stop it now, will you? My vacuum cleaner's broken and my boys are trying to make a snowman out of your—'

Before she could finish, there was another knock at the door. Mouse didn't want to leave the room. Firstly because he was too captivated by Dan's powers, and also because he couldn't see where the door was any more. But with Mum rounding up the twins before they built the most rancid snowman in history, he staggered from the room, noticing the weirdest eggy smell as he went. When he opened the front door, the smell got worse. Much worse. And there on the doorstep was another stranger, maybe sixteen years old, wearing jeans and a puffer jacket. Whatever Mouse was smelling, it didn't seem to be troubling this kid. His grin was wide and welcoming.

'You're Mouse,' he said. 'I saw you on the news. The name's Mark.'

'You'd better come in,' Mouse gasped, hoping he could trap the worst of the whiff on the far side of the door.

'This is Mark, everyone,' Mouse announced. A number of

introductions and handshakes followed, as well as the wrinkling of noses at the whiff that wouldn't go away.

Mouse couldn't wait to get to the big question.

'So can you do something, Mark? he asked. 'Because you won't believe what Dan here can do. Not that it matters, you're welcome anyway.'

'Not sure if I can impress anyone,' Mark said sheepishly. 'Not many people appreciate what I can do. No one, in fact. I don't even have a superhero name. Couldn't think of—' At that moment, Mark stopped abruptly, and without warning, let rip with the loudest bottom burp that anyone in the room had ever heard. So savage was its volume that it shook the pictures on the wall, and its backdraft made the door slam shut. What followed was even more terrifying, as slowly, a smell that can only be described as evil started to circulate, nipping at the nostrils before punching and kicking them into submission.

Mouse's imagination was going mental. What if he could bottle that smell? He could make the world's deadliest stinkbombs. Smash one in a maths exam and bingo! School would be cancelled for a week!

'Sweet mercy!' yelled Mum as she dived to open the windows. 'What have you been eating, Mark?'

'Nothing dodgy, I gave up sprouts years ago when my mum
threatened to have me adopted. I can't help it.'

That was as may be, but it didn't help matters. Cyclots was
wretching, while Dan shook his head to try and help his senses
escape the whiff, which merely brought about another snow
storm. The twins started moaning and the triplets suddenly
decided they'd had enough too.

'I'm sorry, I'm sorry!' Mark wailed and let rip with another
series of guffs that this time verged on the musical, as they
climbed a series of notes.

Down on the floor, Bruce heard the rasping tune, stopped
crying and began to giggle. Peter looked at his brother and
started to do the same. Clark, not wanting to miss out followed
suit, and within seconds the twins were giggling too.

'That's amazing,' Mouse said, laughing. 'It normally takes us ages to stop them crying. Did you know you could fart a tune?'

'Oh, yeah, though it takes a lot of focus. One wrong note can have terrible consequences.'

'Play us another one then,' Mouse said, holding his nose in anticipation.

Mark pondered for a second, then let fly with the most miraculous version of the Superman theme tune. There was more laughter from the babies, plus shrieks of delight. Even Mum was amused, hanging out of the window and gasping for air as her shoulders shook with laughter.

'I've got it.' Mouse yelled. 'I know what your hero name should be. It's obvious. From now on, you will be known as . . . THE SKIDMARK!'

There was a unanimous chorus of agreements, following by one final almighty guff, which had Mark asking for directions to the loo.

Mouse smiled as he showed him the way. Who'd have thought it? His own merry league of superheroes. All right, they might have been a pound shop version of The Avengers, but at that moment, Mouse didn't care a bit. He'd never, ever, been happier.

Word Gets Around

Word of Mouse and Mum's new friends travelled faster than
a greedy man round a sweet shop. Little wonder, really. Storey
Street was a smallish road, and to be honest, Mouse's band of
merry men were an unusual feast upon the eye. A giant, a man
who guffed with practically every step and the world's flakiest
scalp were never going to go unnoticed, especially when they
were spotted with Seacross's latest celebrities.

Mouse could tell Mum was surprised to see the trio waiting
by the front gate when they opened the door for school, but not
unhappy. The three visitors had proved themselves more than
useful the night before, especially when she was finally putting
the boys to bed.

While Mum had bathed the triplets, Cyclots spotted that the
Bratmobile had a slow puncture and patched it up. He'd also
given the buggy a full service, making it run smoother than a

souped-up Ferrari.

Dan hadn't sat on his backside either. Seeing that the kitchen resembled the inside of a wheelie bin, he'd flicked on the radio, found a station playing heavy metal music, and set about the washing up. Mouse giggled as his new ally began to dance, though he'd insisted Dan wore a shower cap, as any sudden head-banging would lead to a storm of Antarctic proportions.

The Skidmark proved to be the biggest success of the evening. Mum and Mouse always dreaded getting the five boys into bed – it was an endless game of ping-pong as they dashed from bedroom to bedroom, shushing and cooing, knowing that one scream or yell would set the other four off again.

Not last night, though, for as Mum gave the twins their bath, Mark managed the unthinkable. He got the triplets to sleep. In minutes.

'How did you do it?' Mum whispered, awestruck. 'You didn't gas them, did you?'

'Course not!' he said, smiling. 'Lullabies. Want me to work my magic on the twins too?'

Mouse's brain flashed back to Dad leaning over his brothers' cots, singing softly as his own eyelids drooped with tiredness. It made Mouse miss him, though he refused to let the thought settle. Dad had made his choice, hard as it was to accept.

Mum looked as if she was about to cry with joy and Mark looked pretty chuffed too as he tucked Dean and Roger in. Slowly and with great tenderness, he'd started to hum, and 'Rock-a-bye Baby' filled the room. Its effect was mesmerising! The boys couldn't take their eyes off him, but at the same time were fighting the heaviness of their eyelids. Within minutes, resistance was futile, and their chests rose and fell dreamily. Mark turned to face Mum and Mouse, still humming, although his mouth was wide and smiling.

Hang on? Mouse thought. How was he humming if his mouth was open?

EUGH!

The truth hit him. Just before the smell did.

Oh. My. Days.

If this guy could gently fart five boisterous boys into a sleepy submission, then there were no limits to his powers. And if he didn't make it as a superhero? Well, he could make a fortune on the stage. People would pay good money to listen to The Skidmark's tuneful bottom. (Though they wouldn't want to smell it.)

Mark didn't brag or make a fuss as he passed them at the

doorway. He headed straight for the bathroom and gently closed the door. Mum and Mouse beat a hasty retreat before things got nasty.

The rest of the evening was lovely. Mum got teary when she saw the buggy and the kitchen, and thanked all three of them about a hundred and fifty times in the next three and a half minutes.

'Don't be silly,' Cyclots had replied. 'It's us who should be thanking you. If I hadn't seen how brave you were, I'd still be sitting at home, dreaming of a pencil-sharpening promotion. Instead I'm here, with people just like me. And it feels magic!'

'We don't want to be a pain,' added Dan. 'But maybe we can help you a bit. You know, with cleaning and the kids. Just when you're feeling overwhelmed.'

Well, that had really set Mum's tear ducts off and they'd spent the next hour drinking tea and passing endless tissues. In the end, Mouse had told her to pull herself together. You never saw Bruce Wayne blubbing to Robin over the state of the Batcave!

Thankfully, there were no tears on the way to school today, though there were oodles of raised eyebrows, giggles and enquiring looks from parents and classmates.

Cyclots, Dan-Druff and The Skidmark had all added capes to their costumes overnight (well, a selection of grubby tablecloths and sun-bleached curtains anyway) and they looked mighty impressive as they helped Mum at the crossing. It was a windy December day, and the wind made their capes billow and dance to great dramatic effect.

At school, Mouse faced endless questions about his new comrades.

'Where are they from?'

'How did they acquire their powers?'

'Was that tall one wearing a tablecloth?'

Just like yesterday, this was exactly the attention Mouse had craved for years. He was in his element – even if he was sometimes vague with his answers. He didn't want to spoil the sense of mystery and wonder – and he certainly didn't want to tell them about Cyclots's other career at the pencil factory.

The one question he *did* have to answer properly came from Jake and Floss.

'So if you're this group of superheroes, what are you called?' asked Floss.

'Yeah,' added Jake. 'Are you part of the X-Men, then? Or, like, a second division Avengers?'

It was a good question, and one that, unbelievably, Mouse didn't already have an amazing answer ready for. He knew it had to be something original and memorable . . . something that summed them up neatly.

Thankfully, help was nearby, in the shape of an eavesdropping Masher Milner.

'Huh,' he groaned. 'Avengers? Your bunch of zeroes? As if!'

Mouse's ears pricked up. 'That's right, Masher. We are zeroes. That's what makes us different, that's what makes us . . . *The Z-List!*'

Mouse liked how it sounded as it tripped off his tongue. A bit like the X-Men, but further down the alphabet. It had mystery and intrigue.

By the time the bell rang for the end of school, everyone wanted to be introduced to the town's newest vigilantes properly, and piled out to the zebra crossing, where the unsuspecting trio were waiting – even Nigel who'd taken a rare day off from his beloved pencils.

What followed was unexpected, ridiculous and absolutely great fun. Cyclots, Dan-Druff and The Skidmark lapped up the attention from their scrum of new fans, answering every question and request for autographs with delight. Then they let them all follow them back to Mouse's house, where they proceeded to hold a kind of 'Z-List show' in the back garden.

Mouse, leading the way, couldn't have been happier. He felt like the Pied Piper in a cape . . . and goggles.

Right now, Cyclots had a queue of people with broken bikes to fix, Dan-Druff was busy creating enough flakes for kids to build their own dandruff sculptures, while The Skidmark had dozens of frazzled mothers waiting in line for him to guff their babies gently to sleep.

The real highlight came later in the afternoon, at the expense of Masher and his friends, who, true to form, were out to gatecrash and make trouble.

Mum had managed to rustle up some bowls of crisps and biscuits (Mouse didn't know where from), but Masher decided that sharing was for wimps.

As the bullies settled round the garden table, pushing the other kids out of the way, Mouse watched with glee while The Skidmark and Dan-Druff crept up behind them, and Cyclots approached from the front.

'Lovely day, isn't it?' Cyclots said, beaming at Masher, who grunted a reply through a gobful of crisps. 'There's going to be an eclipse later, you know.'

Masher, Saliva and Bunions all looked away from their stolen treats and up towards the sun. While they were distracted, Dan leaned over them and started nodding his head like a salt shaker so that flake after flake of dandruff fell into their crisps unnoticed.

The three bullies didn't even realise what had happened until they'd finished the whole bowl.

'What flavour were they?' grimaced Masher, feeling the onset of a belly ache.

'Dunno,' said Saliva. 'I thought they were bacon at first, but they were way too salty for that. I've not had anything like them before.'

Mouse laughed so hard his head was in danger of falling off, especially when all three of them started to turn an unsightly shade of green.

'I feel weird,' Masher groaned.

'Me too,' said Saliva.

'And me,' said Bunions.

Behind them, The Skidmark emptied his guts with a silent yet deadly rasp that turned their bellies even further.

'I feel . . . '

' . . . sick.'

Within seconds, Masher, Saliva and Bunions were on their feet and dashing towards the gate.

This is the business! thought Mouse. *Who'd have thought that being a powerless superhero could possibly be so much fun?* Little did Mouse know that he hadn't seen anything yet . . .

Behind him, another figure in a cape swept effortlessly through the side gate.

The woman's purple leather costume and mask were so sleek and shiny it was impossible to ignore, as was the cape, which looked as if it had been spun by an army of silkworms. Through the masses the woman strode, the heels of her knee-high leather boots echoing loudly on the paving. There were gasps and ooohs of wonder from everyone in the garden, and a buzz of anticipation as she finally stood, motionless, hands upon her hips.

'I,' she said, in a voice as silky as her cape, 'am Vortex! Watch me work!'

With a flourish, she threw both of her arms in front of her, fingers outstretched as a thunderous noise kicked in, loud enough to drown out even the most savage Skidmark fart.

What happened next was extraordinary. It was as if every vacuum cleaner on Storey Street had been turned on at once, creating the most incredible tornado of suction. Bushes and trees started to sway and bend, dead leaves were sucked clean off the lawn and whipped through the air in Vortex's direction.

A Bunch of Suckers . . .

Mouse watched in wonder as the particles span dizzily towards Vortex's wrists, and up two discreet tubes that disappeared inside her leather sleeves. It was a seriously impressive piece of kit.

Mouse scooted closer, clocking that the tubes fed into a large rucksack which sat beneath her cape.

Everything about her screamed SUPERHERO, and she knew it.

So did the crowd, who erupted into yells of admiration the second she let her arms fall back to her sides.

'Thank you, my friends, thank you.' She beamed. 'I'm here to serve you. If you'll have me. If you will let me be one of you.' She pointed in The Z-List's direction.

Cyclots, Dan-Druff and The Skidmark didn't complain. They had all fallen hopelessly and instantly in love. Mum was gobsmacked too. Imagine what this newcomer could do for her grubby carpets?

What could Mouse say?

Nothing.

All he could do was gawp and shake Vortex's gloved hand.
If she was for real, then The Z-List really meant business. Storey
Street had never been safer. It was so safe, Mouse thought they
should rename it Superhero Street.

It had also never been shinier. Every kerb and hedgerow
squeaked with cleanliness, even the pigeons had a shine to them,
and it was all thanks to the magnificent, all-powerful, Vortex.
The newest member of The Z-List was a smash hit and much in
demand.

'Would you clean my kitchen . . ?'

' . . . my car?'

' . . . my children?'

But while Cyclots would repair every single bicycle wheeled in front of him, The Vortex wasn't quite as obliging.

'It's kind of you to ask,' she told one father with an attic that needed a spring clean, 'But a superhero must rest. What would happen if aliens were to attack when my powers were drained?'

The man looked to the heavens with a baffled look on his face. If UFOs were to visit Earth, he was sure the last place they'd come was Seacross. They'd go to Dullsville and Yawnstown before they hovered over these streets.

For some reason, though, the one house The Vortex couldn't wait to get inside was Mouse's.

'What a wonderful looking place,' she said on her second visit. 'I'd love to have a guided tour.'

Mouse frowned. Vortex was a bit full-on. He loved their home, but it was just a terraced house. And a scuzzy one at that. There were dozens of them in better condition, up and down the length of Storey Street.

Mum was feeling far more hospitable. It might have been the presence (finally) of a fellow female 'superhero' or it might have been the prospect of a house that shone brighter than the sun, but either way, Mum was delighted to usher Vortex inside.

This was, of course, a HUGE mistake, as you and I, readers, (or at least, the sharper ones among us) know, that The Vortex isn't really a superhero at all. She is none other than Esther D'astardly, hellbent on finding the priceless diamond lodged in the changing bag on the back of the Bratmobile.

Shocking, I know, but true. The last of Esther's ill-gotten riches had been spent on the elaborate suction system and sleek costume. All she had to do now was fool this woeful Wonderwoman wannabe and her stupid sidekick of a son, locate the canvas bag, pilfer its contents and head straight for the airport.

But Mouse wasn't as stupid as Esther thought. Nearly, but not quite. He might have been dazzled his entire life by the glamour of being a superhero, but when, finally, a properly impressive one landed on his doorstep, he didn't quite know what to make of it.

Vortex was just too slick. She wasn't real like the rest of them. She hadn't told them her real name. She didn't even seem to have a job like Cyclots.

'How did she get her hands on a suction machine like that?' he asked The Skidmark, as Mum showed Vortex into the kitchen.

'Dunno,' he answered. 'She probably invented it. She looks properly clever.'

Mouse didn't doubt it, but it must have cost a fortune. People in Seacross didn't usually have that sort of money, and if they did, they used it for important inventions like chocolate hot water bottles and two-storey bungalows.

'And I'd love to know where that costume came from,' he said to Dan.

'Mine came from the tea towel drawer,' Dan answered, stroking his tatty stained cape. 'Belonged to my gran, this tablecloth.'

He wasn't sure why, but Dan's reply summed up exactly what was bothering Mouse. Vortex looked like she'd stepped straight out of the silver screen, while the rest of The Z-List had a straight-to-DVD look about them.

What was she really doing here?

The thought made Mouse's head itchier than Dan-Druff's, but with nothing to go on except a hunch, he was left trailing Mum and their guest from room to room, just in case he could get a clearer sense of what she was all about.

Vortex was saying all the right things:

'Aren't the rooms a good size?'

'Warm too . . . '

'Oh, that duvet cover is glorious . . . '

But Mouse couldn't help noticing that her eyes seemed to be analysing everything in the room rather than appreciating them – as if she was trying to locate something very specific. What that might be, Mouse had no idea. Still, maybe he was just being paranoid.

When they returned to the kitchen, Vortex's eyes widened as she spotted Cyclots hard at work with the Bratmobile.

'My word,' she exclaimed, shoving Mouse aside and dashing towards the buggy.

'What a feat of engineering this is!'

'Oh, aye,' said Cyclots. 'Though it's a beggar for flat tyres. I only fixed this one yesterday and it's shredded already. Still, hardly a surprise given the weight it's carrying!'

Vortex laughed. A shrill, false noise, the kind you heard in response to a crummy Christmas cracker joke, Mouse thought. She circled the buggy, eyes flicking over every part of it. She looked at it from every angle, above, beneath, at one point she looked set to climb into the seats and buckle herself in. But after the sixth lap, the laughter faded, and her grinning face crumbled into something more creased and irritable.

'Anything wrong?' Mouse asked. He really didn't understand why she was acting so strangely.

'Wrong?' She grimaced at him, before pasting on another smile. 'Wrong? What could possibly be wrong, when here I am, surrounded by people just like me? Every second I get to spend with you is an absolute joy.'

Mouse frowned. He didn't like how that last word sounded as it came out. It sounded as if Vortex's mouth was full of broken glass and barbed wire.

He was the only one to pick up on it, though.

'You like the buggy, Vortex?' Mum asked. 'It used to be the twins', before we customised it for the triplets.'

'Like it? I love it. It's just so roomy. It looks like the sort of contraption that would have lots of secret compartments. You know, places where you could hide, I don't know, for sake of an argument, a canvas bag. One that might hold nappies and wipes and dia . . . ' Vortex bit her lip suddenly.

'Not really. I just hook a bag on the back,' said Mum.

'But you must have to carry such a lot of nappies with five beautiful babies to think of,' said Vortex.

Mouse's frown was now the size of Russia. What on earth was she going on about? Why was an uber-cool vigilante banging on endlessly about nappies?

'Oh, it takes endless planning,' Mum replied. 'I must have dozens of different change bags dotted around the house. I really should get on top of them and condense it down into one.'

'Why don't I do that for you over the next day or so?' Vortex said. 'I could give the house a good once over while I'm at it, vacuum the curtains and carpets. No point having these gifts and not using them to do good!'

Mouse had heard enough. He didn't trust Vortex – she was hiding something, he was sure of it. Besides, *he* hadn't become a superhero to clean the house. He wanted to help people, not polish them within an inch of their life.

Grumbling, he walked away. He'd actually rather clean out the bottom of Frederico's cage than listen to her any more.

Every Laser Wins . . .

Crazes come and go quickly in school playgrounds. In my day it was conkers and marbles (I know, I know, I don't look old enough, do I?) and now it's trading cards and fancy apps that must be powered by some kind of crazy witchcraft.

Within a week of The Z-List forming, there was only one craze sweeping the halls of Storey Street Junior School – and that was an unadulterated worship of all things 'Z'.

Students sported DIY capes and costumes, one kid had poured a whole bag of flour into his hair so he could be just like Dan. It was rumoured that the headmaster, Mr Peach, had acquired a tattoo of a winged lollipop stick on his shoulder, but nobody dared ask him if it was true. Although he did blush furiously whenever he saw Mouse's mum.

Things on Storey Street were peaceful. Crime was at an all-time low, which was saying something, since it was already almost non-existent. No one dared drop litter on the street out of fear of Vortex. And no one fell off their bikes either as, thanks to Cyclots, they all ran smoother than the Bratmobile itself.

Every day, The Z-List were a welcome presence, sometimes pumping up tyres, sometimes pumping out a tune, and whatever they were doing, they were loved for it.

Mouse should have been super-chuffed, and he was, he wasn't an ungrateful kid – and this was what he'd always wanted in life. To be seen, and seen as special. But at the same time, he couldn't ignore the fact that something was missing. And that something was Dad.

What made it worse for our poor hero was that he didn't know if he was allowed to miss Dad. After all, Dad had walked out on them. Mum couldn't hear his name without either looking cross or close to tears. Mouse was angry with Dad, sure, sometimes he felt like he hated him even. But at the same time, he missed watching Dad teaching him the tricks of his mystical trade. He even missed the sound of him snoring on the sofa.

'I shouldn't feel lonely,' he kept saying to himself. 'I've all these new pals now.' And it was true. The house had never been fuller, or cleaner. But somehow it still wasn't the same.

Vortex, for some reason, had taken it upon herself to show up every day, simply to suck the dust from all corners of the house. The woman was a cleaning machine! But another weird thing about her was that instead of finishing a room with a satisfied sigh of achievement, as Mum did when she was cleaning, Vortex would become more and more irate. Her eyes would flick from sofa to fireplace to window, as if she was still searching for a rogue speck of dust. And when she couldn't find one, it sent her into a rage.

'Inconceivable,' she'd mutter and spit. 'How difficult can it be?'

Mouse always wanted to answer when she said that. Didn't Vortex realise it WAS difficult for Mum to keep a clean house when she was on her own with six kids? He never did, of course, he was too well mannered, he'd been *brought* up, not *dragged* up (as Mum always said). He just bit his tongue and said nothing, though he would scream if Vortex stepped foot on his loft ladder. He didn't like the idea of her cleaning his stuff. Knowing her, she'd paint over the comic strip on his walls.

He watched her day after day, turning up out of the blue to vacuum and tidy with a greater and greater fever. She never bothered joining the others on the school run, despite being encouraged to.

'I really want to finish this room,' she'd snap, before recovering her smile. 'If you don't mind. It would mean a lot to me. To be able to help you, that is.'

Mum never minded – she was eternally grateful to all of The Z-List. 'I don't know how I'd have coped without you,' she said.

Mouse couldn't help sneering. He loved his new friends dearly, but there was one of them he could definitely live without.

One morning, about a week after forming, the rest of The Z-List set off for school – an almighty sight, high-fiving every schoolchild and parent they passed. As they approached, Mouse spotted a huge crowd gathering at the gates. Instantly, his senses went to high alert, as did his excitement levels.

'Keep your eyes peeled,' he said gravely to Dan, Mark and Cyclots. 'This may be a situation for us to diffuse.'

The threesome reacted speedily. Cyclots pulled his cycling shorts up, Dan shook a storm of scalp to the ends of hair, and The Skidmark tooted something that sounded strangely like the theme tune to Coronation Street.

Getting closer, however, Mouse realised with great disappointment that the threat level was minimal. As soon as The

Z-List were spotted, people started to applaud and cheer and whoop. More than that, there was a TV crew present. Mum was quickly confronted by news anchorman, Kyle Ramsbottom.

'Joanna Mouse!' he said, flashing his pearly teeth at her. 'Or should I say Lady Lollipop! I'm here today, in the presence of your family and friends, to bring you wonderful news. In light of your heroism, it has been decided by those on high that you will be granted the highest honour imaginable by this wonderful town of ours. Next Monday, at City Hall, you are to be a VIP at a ceremony where you will be given the keys to Seacross!'

Blimey, thought Mouse. *This was amazing!*

He'd always wondered what getting the keys to a town actually meant. Would Mum get a massive keyring that gave her access to every house, shop and office in the whole of Seacross? That was generous, but wouldn't it be a bit weird for people if they were sitting in their lounge watching telly, only for Mouse and Mum to barge in and raid the biscuit tin? He wasn't sure he'd like it.

'Well, what do you think?' Kyle added.

'I don't know what to say . . . ' gasped Mum.

'We do,' said Cyclots, laughing.

'She'd be honoured!' added Dan-Druff.

'It'll be a night to remember, for all of us,' said Mouse.

And do you know what? He was absolutely right. But not for the reasons he imagined.

The Keys to the Kingdom

The Z-List looked like a squazillion dollars. OK, so they might not have been glamorous enough to be mistaken for A-Listers, but you can't really turn a man with dandruff as bad as Dan's into George Clooney, not with only the use of a flannel and a twenty-five quid Topman voucher. But they were definitely higher up the alphabet than 'Z' now.

'P'. Maybe even 'N', but not 'L'. Not quite.

Cyclots had invested in new cycling kit, complete with LED lights that flashed his name across his chest, Dan-Druff's hair was especially flaky, after not being washed for a week, and The Skidmark had bought a new pair of boxer shorts with a reinforced gusset. This was monumental news, since for the past year and a half his pants had been held together with an equal measure of luck and prayer. Mouse and Mum had turned out smartly too. Mum's lollipop uniform and stick shone fluorescently, while Mouse had invested in some new goggles that didn't steam up the second he put them on over his specs.

The only person who hadn't made a special effort was Vortex, who'd been keen to stay home and finish cleaning the back bedroom. Mum was having none of it.

'You're one of us now,' she'd said. 'And anyway, you always look so smart, you don't need to dress up!'

Vortex had smiled through gritted teeth and reluctantly joined them.

Through the immense crowd at City Hall The Z-List strode, signing autographs, offering advice on slow punctures and scalp hygiene (or lack of it). The triplets and twins were having an amazing time, watching in wide-eyed wonder from the Bratmobile as everyone came to meet them.

'Ladies and Gentlemen!' rasped a voice through the loudspeakers. 'Can I ask you to take your seats, as our ceremony is about to begin!'

Obediently the crowd dispersed, leaving our heroes to climb the steps to the stage. There was a seat for each of them up there – at Mum's insistence, even though she was the only one being honoured – and even a playpen and toys to occupy the babies. No detail had been left ignored, not if it made Lady

Lollipop and her team happy. Mouse felt like he was living one of his comic book dreams.

There was always the scene, on the last page, where the hero would stand before a crowd to accept their adulation: that moment when a medal was proudly pinned to their chest. And now Mouse was going to see that happen to his own mum, for real.

The ceremony began with a speech from ruddy-faced Mayor and local butcher, Stanley Albertson, who looked as if he'd spent the last forty years eating sausages instead of selling them. It wasn't the most riveting piece of public speaking. Mouse turned off after twenty-five minutes, scouring the hall for potential threats to neutralise. Not that he found a lot to concern him, apart from Masher Milner and pals making rude hand gestures in his direction from row Q.

Instead of worrying about those dozy planks he turned back to the Mayor, who was now brandishing the poshest-looking lollipop stick Mouse had ever seen in his life.

'As a mark of respect and thanks for your bravery, the people of Seacross would like to present you, Joanna Mouse, AKA Lady Lollipop, with this limited edition, gold-plated lollipop stick. May it help you keep us safe for many years to come.'

Mum didn't seem to know what to say. Mainly because she was so dazzled by the reflection bouncing off her gift – the head of the stick was littered with glistening gems and rubies (plastic), and the stick itself was alternated with gold and silver effect stripes. It must have cost a lot – ooooh, a good sixty quid at least – to make. No expense had been spared.

'But aside from this beautiful memento, we are here to bestow on you the greatest honour imaginable, the keys to our town, and the freedom of Seacross.'

From an ornate padded box, he pulled a HUGE key ring that must have held well over a hundred different keys. There also seemed to be a fob attached in the shape of someone from One Direction. Mouse felt nauseous. It was hardly classy. Why not choose someone from The Avengers, for Pete's sake?

'From this day forth,' Stanley continued. 'You have the right to drive a herd of sheep through our streets whenever you wish, to ring the Cathedral bells at a drop of a hat . . . and you are also entitled to twenty per cent off any sausage or pork product from Albertson & Son & Son Butchers. Terms and conditions apply.'

The crowd gasped in wonder – mostly at the final bit of the prize, it was past teatime and bellies were rumbling. Mum looked emotional. She held the keys aloft, and lifted Mouse's hand too,

as he stood proudly beside her, feeling like he'd just saved New York City from the clutches of Dr Well'Ard.

As the ceremony ended, half the hall approached them for photos and autographs, and they obliged with the grace of experienced, seasoned heroes. Not faring quite so well, though, were Mouse's brothers, who with bedtime looming, had kicked off in spectacular fashion. It was so noisy among their fans that even the calming tunes of The Skidmark's bottom couldn't soothe them. Mouse knew that unless they were out of there and into bed quick-smart, there would be tears and tantrums of epic proportions.

But when Mum announced she was leaving, it was met with consternation (a posh word for dismay, and not the collective term for stars as some wallies might tell you).

'You can't do that!' gasped The Skidmark.

'This is your party,' agreed Cyclots.

'And I've ten kilos of sausages about to be served . . . ' moaned Stanley Albertson.

It was Vortex who stepped in with a solution. So keen was she to make it happen that she skipped from foot to foot like a small child in need of a very urgent wee.

'I shall take the boys home,' she said.

'Oh, I couldn't let you do that,' Mum said. 'It's ever so kind of you, but it's not your job. It's mine.'

'Oh, I insist.' Vortex's tone was firm, and there was a fire in her eyes that made Mouse feel a bit weird. 'After all, that's what being in a . . . team means.'

She coughed violently, as if the word 'team' had burned her throat with acid.

Mum still wasn't comfortable with the offer. 'No, it's too much to ask. I struggle to manage it myself.'

'Then I'll go with her,' said Cyclots.

'Me too,' said The Skidmark.

'And me,' added Dan-Druff.

Their generosity made Mum beam, but not Vortex. Mouse could see her getting more and more agitated by the second. Why did she want to get back to their house so quickly? And why didn't she want the others to join her?

Mouse had no idea, but he wasn't going to let her leave without him too. His super senses were tingling. And he had to get to the bottom of it.

'Would you mind if I went home too, Mum? All this adoration is a bit tiring, plus if I'm around the boys might settle quicker.'

Mum looked surprised, but didn't get in Mouse's way. Instead, she hugged each of her boys, before being swallowed up by the crowd again.

'Come on,' said Vortex, with a frown. 'Let's get home. There's a lot to do.'

And boy, oh boy, she wasn't kidding . . .

Vortex Comes Clean

People are strange. Believe me, I know.

Some people go their whole lives wearing masks they never allow to slip. The Vortex had kept hers (literally) clamped to her face ever since arriving on the scene, but now it was in danger of sliding off her sweat-soaked nose and onto the floor.

Esther D'astardly was worried – and this worried her. She wasn't the worrying kind. She'd infiltrated the inner sanctum of these idiots over two weeks ago, but there was still no sign of the missing diamond. She'd tidied and zapped every room in the house, some of them five times, including the Mighty Brat's attic lair, and the gem was nowhere to be seen.

Time and again she replayed the day of the robbery in her brain, but each time, the result was the same. She'd seen the diamond fall into a bag on the back of the buggy, she was sure of it. Then where in heaven's name was it?

Time was running out. She daren't return to her hideout any more, after spotting police lurking about. If she wanted to escape to the Caribbean before they finally nicked her, she had to get her hands on that gem. And it had to be tonight.

Wiping the sweat from her cheeks, she ran through her strategy. It was a simple Three Point Plan, but effective:

1. Get the five smaller brats to bed. (Points Two and Three would be easier and quieter that way.)
2. Knock out the three Super-Idiots and tie them up.
3. Torture Mouse until he gave up the location of the diamond.

A lot rested on Point Three, Esther was aware of that, but she believed Mouse knew more than he was letting on. He had to. She'd seen the way he looked at her, all sly and disbelieving. If anyone knew where her fortune was hiding, it was him. He was probably intending to spend it himself on a stack of useless comics, which made her fume. It was hers to fritter away, not his!

So while Cyclots, Dan-Druff, The Skidmark and Mouse wrestled the little ones into bed, Esther laid the groundwork for her plan. First, she soaked the entire kitchen floor with six panfuls of water. Then, with a calmness that only an evil super-villain possesses, she sat and sipped a cup of tea, rising again when she heard the thud of footsteps on the stairs.

'Guys! Guys!' she called in a stage whisper. 'Come quick! There's been a leak under the sink.'

Obediently, the four heroes trotted in her direction, slipping and sliding on the wet lino.

'I've no idea how it started,' she said. 'And I'm no plumber . . . '

Crowding around the kitchen cupboard Cyclots, The SkidMark and Dan-Druff bent down to peer inside, presenting Esther with the opportunity she was waiting for.

Quick as a flash, she whipped a rolling pin from behind her back, and with minimal effort, clonked each of our heroes on the back of the noggin.

They hadn't yet reached the floor before Mouse realised all his doubts and fears were real. Vortex *wasn't* what she seemed, and now she was walking menacingly towards him, rolling pin poised.

Things weren't looking good. Mouse felt a bit like David probably had when he'd first spotted Goliath, except Mouse didn't have either a slingshot in his hand, or free arms to launch any kind of attack.

Esther D'astardly had tied him securely to the kitchen chair, using almost a full roll of sticky tape in the process. She'd tried to find some rope in the shed, and you should have heard the language when she was unsuccessful. Mouse had no idea what most of the words meant, and doubted Mum would either to be honest. Not that he'd dare ask her.

Vortex had done a similar job on the other, still unconscious, Z-Listers, improvising when the tape finally ran out. Poor Skidmark had his legs tied together with a pair of oven gloves, Dan-Druff was bound by a dressing gown

cord, while Cyclots was restrained by a pair of tights and the elastic from Mum's best pair of pants. Into each of their mouths, she'd jammed a pair of socks, but not Mouse's.

'Now listen here, you little runt. I want answers, and I want them quick. So tell me, where is it?' she said.

Mouse frowned, confused. 'Where's what?'

'Don't play the innocent with me. I knew you were cleverer than the others, which isn't saying much, but I knew the second I saw you. So tell me where you've hidden it and this will all be over peacefully.'

Mouse's head span. He had no idea what Vortex was going on about, although if anything had been hidden it was her manners. Somehow, though, he didn't think she was hunting for those.

'I don't know what you're talking about, but I'm guessing your name isn't really Vortex and that you don't really want to be a superhero at all!' he said.

Esther laughed, a laugh as dastardly as her surname. 'Well, you're right about that, you little maggot. The last two weeks have been hell. Listening to you and your lapdogs bang on about being super, when I've seen more power in an empty battery.'

Ouch! That insult hurt Mouse more than the tape digging into his wrists.

'I'm going to ask you one more time,' snarled Esther, finally whipping off the Vortex mask to reveal her true identity. 'Where. Is. The. Diamond?'

Mouse didn't mean to gasp, but he couldn't help it. I mean, here were two massive revelations. He didn't want Esther to know that he recognised her off the News – but he was only ten, and even the toughest superheroes get scared sometimes. Why hadn't he seen through her disguise? Her face had been on the telly practically every day since the robbery . . . So why, as this budding superhero, hadn't he been able to spot her through a teeny tiny mask? Looking around at his unconscious friends, Mouse felt ashamed.

'So. Are you going to spill the beans?' Esther said. 'Or do I have to get *really* nasty?'

Mouse didn't want her to get nasty, 'course he didn't. He was just overwhelmed by the fact that there was a precious jewel hiding somewhere in their house, and even more overwhelmed that Esther hadn't found it after all her rigorous cleaning!

Panicking at the torture he imagined stretched out before him, he racked his brain for where this diamond could possibly be lurking. But no matter how hard he thought, he simply didn't have a Scooby Doo.

Panic turned back into fear. What was he going to do? And, more importantly, what was evil Esther going to do to him?!

For the first time since Mum had foiled the robbery, Mouse felt doubts nagging at him – the same ones he'd felt the day Masher had dunked him in the swimming pool. They reminded him he was no kind of hero. That he was the same insignificant, anonymous boy he'd always been. A boy incapable of thwarting a master criminal's sinister plan.

But suddenly, from nowhere, Mouse realised that it didn't matter if he was ordinary. He could pretend not to be. He could play along and make up a hiding place for the diamond, tell Esther D'astardly that it was in his room, somewhere difficult to get to. While she was gone, he'd escape, free the others, grab his brothers and leg it.

Once he'd done that, he'd call the police, who would throw Vortex in prison for a million years and he'd be branded a hero all over again. Perfect!

Without hesitation, he launched the plan into action:

'OK, OK! I hid it. I hid it in my bedroom. Under a loose floorboard, behind the wardrobe. You can have it. I don't want it. All I want is for you to let us go!'

Esther smiled slyly. 'That's more like it. Now I'm going to go upstairs and retrieve my diamond . . . But I warn you, Mouse, that while I'm gone, if you try and escape, free the others, grab your brothers, leg it and call the police in the vain hope that they will throw me in prison for million years, then . . . then . . . '

Mouse felt a lump of what was possibly vomit collect in his throat. ' . . . then I will be very VERY unhappy.'

With a swift, sinister movement, she leaned forwards, shoved a sock into Mouse's mouth, and ran from the kitchen, shutting the door behind her.

Instantly Mouse went into overdrive. He reckoned he had about fifteen minutes before Esther heaved the heavy wardrobe aside, realised the diamond wasn't there and returned to exact her revenge. But it was hard to think clearly with a sock wedged so far inside his mouth that it was tickling his brain.

He tried to fight against the sticky tape, but it wouldn't budge. He tried to spit out the sock to shout at the others to wake up, but every time he tried he almost swallowed the thing. He even tried to tip his chair over in the hope it would break in the fall and he could wriggle free, but he couldn't even manage that.

Instead, he did the only thing that he could do. He sat, with a sock in his mouth, and he cried.

Then, as the hundredth tear dripped off his chin, he heard a key in the front door. Was it Mum? Oh my word, he hoped so. But then again, it was only an hour since they'd left the party. What if Esther wasn't working alone? What if her brother had broken out of prison and had a key? What if he was even worse-tempered than she was?

He heard the door close quietly in the hall, and footsteps move ominously towards the kitchen. His heart felt as if an elephant wearing concrete wellies was trampolining on it.

Please be Mum, please be Mum, please be Mum . . .

The door handle turned.

The door swung open.

And a face appeared that didn't belong to Mum.

It didn't belong to Esther's accomplice either. At least Mouse very much doubted it.

'DNNDNMMM!' yelled Mouse. Which, if he hadn't had a sock in his mouth, would've come out as, 'DAD!'

Because, yes, you've heard right. Dad, Marvin the Magnificent, had chosen this moment to recognise the error of his ways and come home to say sorry.

He didn't say that now, of course. What he actually said was,

'Mouse! What's on earth is going o . . . '

But he didn't get chance to finish his sentence.

Not because he'd fallen asleep though. No, his sentence had no full stop because he'd just been hit over the head by Esther's rolling pin.

Mouse's hope was dashed as quickly as it had arrived. And looking at Dad, lying unconscious on the floor, it was almost as if he'd never been away.

All Tied Up

Kitchens are supposed to be the heart of any home. A cosy place where families gather at the end of a long day to sit and share a meal, or tell each other stories.

Well, Mouse's kitchen was definitely cosy – it was hard not to be with five bodies in it, all tied up and sweaty – but there wasn't much in the way of conversation going on. It wasn't really possible if you were:

A. unconscious

or

B. choking on a sweaty sock

Esther D'astardly had disappeared again after binding Dad to a chair with the washing line. She'd been in such a rush, she hadn't bothered to remove the pants and vests attached to it and now Dad looked like a sedated clothes horse.

Mouse didn't have time to worry about appearances. He reckoned he had five minutes tops until Esther stopped searching for the diamond and returned in a *really* filthy mood. And, to be honest, even if he had *five days*, he didn't think he'd be able to escape.

First things first, he HAD to get the sock out of his mouth. If he could do that, he could call out, try and wake the others from their stupors.

Steeling himself, Mouse did the only thing he could. He started to chew on the sock. It wasn't an easy thing to do. I mean, have you ever tried to eat a sock? Really? You have? Weird . . .

His mouth tasted of washing powder and toenail clippings, but on Mouse went, only stopping when he'd mashed enough of it to spit the mess onto the kitchen floor. He wanted to vomit, but instead he gasped at the air before shouting,

'Dad! Dan-Druff! Skidmark! Cyclots!' To an outsider, this would sound like the ramblings of a madman who lived on the Planet Wibble, but Mouse wasn't bonkers. He had the beginnings of a plan, and he just needed one of his friends – any of them – to wake up.

Again and again he hissed their names, and was on the point of giving up when there was a snort from the lanky frame of Cyclots. With a grunt, the big man's eyes opened, though they looked far from focused.

'Cyclots!' Mouse said. 'I need you to listen. You have to help get us out of this mess.'

Cyclots was bemused. He had no idea where he was, why his head hurt, or why he was suddenly sitting next to a magician in a sparkly tuxedo and bow tie. But he could also see that his friend was upset, and so held his questions in.

'Can you move your legs?' Mouse asked him.

Cyclots nodded. 'From the knee down I can. That's where your Mum's pant elastic finishes.' He looked embarrassed to say it. Like he'd been caught wearing them himself.

'Good,' said Mouse. 'I need you to stretch them out as far as you can.'

'Why?'

'See those cages under the table? Can you use your feet and open as many of them as you can? Think you can do it?'

'I can try,' said Cyclots and, shaking away the dazed birds that circled his head, he stretched out his long, bony left leg.

Mouse watched intently. It wasn't much of a plan, but he

reckoned that if Cyclots could release the menagerie of Dad's animals from their cages, then they might create enough chaos to put Esther off her rampaging stride and give them a lifeline.

So while Cyclots wrapped his toes round the bars, Mouse turned his attention back to waking the others.

'Dad!' he whispered, getting louder with every attempt. But Dad slept on. Mouse was getting more and more worried. Why wouldn't he wake up? Suddenly, he knew what to do. There was no way Dad would sleep through this.

'Dad. Dad. Big news from Mum. You'll never guess what? She's pregnant again!!'

Marvin the Magnificent bolted upright in his chair, eyes flaring with panic.

'What!' he yelled, before wincing in pain at the bump on his head. 'She's not, is she?'

'Bloomin' heck, I hope not,' Mouse answered.

'What's going on? Dad groaned. 'Why am I tied up, and who in the name of Houdini are these three?'

Mouse sighed and quickly gave him the basics about The Z-List and the psychotic armed robber upstairs. Dad took it as well as any middle-aged concussed magician could. In fact, he quickly came up with an idea to help. So good that Mouse felt a bit resentful. It wasn't fair that Dad had deserted them for weeks, only to come back and possibly save the day. Mouse was supposed to be the hero round here.

With a grimace, he swallowed his pride and let Dad continue.

'Mr Cyclots?' Dad asked politely. 'Do you think you can reach the largest cage at the far end?'

Cyclots craned his head around, then nodded with supreme confidence. Slowly but surely he extended his leg like a steel tape measure, all the way to the cage, and with the deftest of nudges from his big toe, unhooked the cage door.

From inside the bars there was a rustling. The door squeaked open, and out hopped Frederico the rabbit, eyes widening at the sight of his long-lost master.

Dad looked as pleased as his pet, and beckoned the bunny over with a series of whistles and coos. 'That's it, boy. Come this way. Come and sit on Mousey. On his lap.' Frederico obediently did as he was told.

'OK, Freddy. Dinnertime,' Dad added, when the rabbit was plonked on Mouse's knee.

'Dad?' said Mouse, worried. 'What do you mean 'dinner time'?' He didn't fancy being a three course meal to a rabbit who over the years had eaten *everything* put in front of him. Whether it was edible or not.

'Look, Mouse. I know you probably don't trust me right now, and I don't blame you, but I know what I'm doing. Honest.'

Mouse thought hard about what Dad was saying. There was no point in staying angry with him if that resulted in everyone being tortured and possibly killed by Esther D'astardly. It would be much better to stay alive. That way he'd have the next two or three months to be REALLY cross with Dad for what he'd done.

Mouse closed his eyes and shivered as he felt Frederico's paws on his chest. He held his breath. What was worse, being tortured by a master criminal, or devoured by a rabbit with the munchies? He was about to find out . . .

Or was he?

No, of course he wasn't. Do you really think I'd do that to you, dear reader, or to Mouse, for that matter? I like him. He's cool. Slightly deluded with all this superhero business, but cool all the same.

Instead of gorging on Mouse's flesh, Frederico set about nibbling the sticky tape wrapped around his chest.

'It's working, Dad, it's working!' Mouse whispered. And it was. With every passing second, Mouse felt his chest expand, the tape pinging loose. Within moments, Frederico had chewed enough of it for Mouse to pull his arms free and rip off the rest. Zipping across the kitchen he untied Dad and Cyclots, and shook the others awake.

Even more importantly, Mouse and his pals' new-found freedom brought with it another plan of epic proportions, as two floors above, they heard a bloodcurdlingly angry scream, followed by the thump of feet on attic steps.

Esther was on her way.

'OK, Z-Listers. Listen up. We have one chance at this, but we *can* do it. We were born to do it . . . '

From Zeroes to Heroes?

Esther D'astardly was fuming. Steaming so hard she looked like a kettle that had been boiling inside a volcano on Mars. (Don't tell me there are no volcanoes on Mars. I do know that – it's just a gag to make the point that she was hopping mad.)

By the time she reached the kitchen door, she was on fire with rage, her brain melting with the multitude of ways she was going to punish Michael J Mouse. Storming into the room, she prowled in front of him. He was right where she'd left him, sitting bolt upright in his chair, the other idiots still unconscious behind. Mouse's cheeks were stuffed with socks, his eyes wide with fear – Esther knew she had him just where she wanted him. There would be no more lies or wild goose chases. In one minute she would know where the diamond was hiding. The boy *had* to know where it was. She was certain of it.

'You think you're smart, don't you?' she sneered. 'With all this hero nonsense? Well, let me tell you, we're about to find out just how super your friends really are. Because if you don't tell me where that diamond is in the next five seconds, I'm going to do the most unspeakably evil things to them. One by one. Using only *this* pencil sharpener. Starting with this idiot.'

She stopped in front of The Skidmark, who was pretending to sleep, the oven gloves tied loosely now around his legs.

Mouse wanted to smile but couldn't. He had to make it look like there was still a sock in his mouth instead of just air. Esther couldn't have picked a better place to start, as Mouse's plan relied on her being as close to The Skidmark as possible.

Mark, squinting through almost closed eyes, felt her presence and, seeing Mouse give the signal, tensed his stomach before pushing with all his worth.

What followed is impossible to put into words. There are no entries in the dictionary that can possibly describe the noise which erupted from The Skidmark's bottom. It had the terror of a Tyrannosaurus rex's roar and the rumble of the 8.22am Intercity train to London.

Let's just say it was deafening, violent and utterly, utterly deadly.

By the time the echo bounced off the walls, Mouse, Cyclots,

Dad and Dan-Druff had all leaped from their chairs and pulled wet handkerchiefs from their pockets, pressing them tightly against their noses and mouths.

Esther turned around, shocked to see her captives free, and even more surprised by the noise invading her eardrums. But as she completed her full rotation, she started to feel disorientated and woozy, which wasn't surprising – you don't let fly with a bottom burp like The Skidmark's without there being a sensory aftermath. The smell was . . . well . . . it was as if someone had taken a rotten fish and hidden it inside a skunk's small intestine for a couple of years, before hanging it on a washing line.

Within thirty seconds Esther's eyes were watering, within a minute her chest was tightening, and after ninety seconds she was holding onto the dining table gasping for air.

'Window!' she gasped desperately. 'Must . . . reach . . . the . . . window.' But with every step she took, there was a Z-Lister in the way, knocking her back.

Time for Phase Two of Mouse's plan.

Pulling the hankie from his mouth momentarily, he yelled, 'Now Dan-Druff, NOW!' And pulled his goggles over his eyes.

Dan wasted no time. He began to shake his head from side to side. The effect was instantaneous and dramatic, the room quickly filling with flakes of scalp. Esther, already gagging on The Skidmark's guff, now had to deal with badly impaired vision too.

No matter how wildly she groped in the blizzard, she could find no trace of Mouse. She staggered blindly, banging into tables and chairs, taking skin off her knees and tainting the already dirty air with her appalling language.

'Now now,' Mouse taunted her from out of the fog. 'Didn't anyone ever tell you that swearing shows a terrible lack of vocabulary?' (It made a change for him to be saying it instead of Mum.)

Esther replied with another volley of obscenities. She was

ripe for the picking, and Mouse knew just how to bring this
to a close.

Ducking through the dandruff cloud, he tapped Cyclots on
the back and told him quietly to sit on one of the chairs. With the
big man in position, he scuttled in front of a disorientated Esther
and, with an almighty shove, pushed her into Cyclots' path. With
great dexterity and speed, especially for a man whose hands and
feet were so far away from his brain, he wrapped his limbs tightly
around the master criminal, binding her with ridiculous ease.

'Blimey,' Mouse shouted in delight. 'How many miles do you
have to cycle to get legs that strong?'

'Not many,' Cyclots replied. 'Though I did wear out six tyres
last week.'

Mouse laughed and after giving the OK to Dan-Druff to stop
snowing, danced around the kitchen, gathering the clothes
line, tights and pants elastic that had bound them only minutes
before.

Throwing them to Dad, he watched as Esther was tied, triple-
strength, to a dining room chair. This wasn't enough for our hero,
though. He knew Esther was as slimy as a toad's holiday home,
so with great delight he bent beneath the table and opened
another of the cages.

Beaming, he walked slowly over to Esther with his hands behind his back.

'Comfortable?' he asked.

'What do you think?' said Esther. She had dandruff clinging to her eyelids. She looked like the world's most pathetic snowman.

'Good. I'd hate for you to be enjoying this,' said Mouse. He made himself walk slowly, savouring the power he felt in every muscle of his body. 'In fact, just in case you do feel in any way comfortable, why don't I let you meet another good friend of mine? I don't *think* she's radioactive, but you never know, one nibble from her, and . . . well you might finally have powers to match those vacuum cleaners on your wrists.' Pulling his hands from behind his back, Mouse gently set Tamara the tarantula down on Esther's lap, and grinned as the spider started to climb her rigid, terrified body.

'I wouldn't recommend any sudden movements,' Mouse sighed. 'It makes her . . . I don't know . . . jumpy.'

He was trying to sound calm, as though he'd expected every bit of his plan to pay off so handsomely all along. Inside, he felt like a badly set jelly. Had they really defeated her?

Behind him, Mouse could hear Dad on the phone to the police, telling them to get here quick. Then, from the hall he heard the slam of a door, and saw Mum appear, her face falling quicker than a brick from the top of the Empire State Building. She didn't seem to know where to look first – at the trail of dandruff destruction covering her kitchen, at the terrified jewel thief tied to her kitchen chair, or at the spineless, responsibility-shy husband who had re-appeared out of nowhere.

Her mouth dropped open but no sound came out.

Instead, she watched Reg the toad hop into the middle of the floor and, without warning, vomit a large, undigested diamond straight onto the floor.

Esther's eyes flared in anger. Mouse couldn't help but laugh. So that's where it was.

And Mum? She just shook her head and wrinkled her nose.

'Has someone guffed in here?' she asked, before tiptoeing her way around the carnage and opening the window.

23

The Bit at the End...

Mouse felt proud. So proud. He could've masterminded world peace, ended global poverty and invented a machine that turned earwax into gold and he wouldn't have been any prouder. There he was, standing on the stage in front of the whole school, surrounded by his fellow Z-Listers.

Two weeks had passed since Vortex's true identity had been exposed, but Mouse had seen more of her on the television than he had of the other three heroes.

Esther's mug appeared on pretty much every News bulletin there was, reunited in court with her brother Ernest as they were sentenced to serve hard time in the crumbling old prison on Seacross's cliffs. As she was led to the police van, the robber turned to the TV cameras, shook her fist and shouted, 'I won't forget what you did, Michael J Mouse!!'

But Mouse wasn't scared or intimidated. By the time Esther

was released she'd have grey hair and chronic arthritis. And as for him? Well, there was no telling how powerful Mouse the Mighty would be by then. He was already untouchable at school, holding crowds in raptures at the tale of how he'd masterminded the greatest fightback since a squazillion aliens tried to turn Planet Earth into their own private swimming pool. (Not that he'd exaggerated any parts of the story.)

Not laying eyes on the other Z-Listers had made Mouse sad, but he understood why it was that way. The other heroes had been in even greater demand since their roles in foiling Esther's plan had come out.

After his bosses read about his part in proceedings, Cyclots finally got his promotion at the factory, which meant longer shifts

and tons of responsibility as he sharpened tens of thousands of pencils every day. He might not have been exercising his legs on his bike as much, but he had new bulging muscles on his fingers that were stronger than many people's arms.

Dan-Druff had been equally busy, hired by scientists as part of a multi-million pound experiment into new high-powered shampoos. It seemed to be working too. Kind of. His hair shone brighter than a saint's reputation, although Mouse did notice he was scratching under his arms a lot. Heaven knows what was growing under there, but Mouse wasn't sure he wanted to find out.

Of all The Z-Listers, The Skidmark had received the most attention. His phone hadn't stopped ringing. Talent spotters from TV shows, record producers wanting to make CDs of his farty lullabies – apparently even the Government had been in touch. They reckoned his iffy guts might be the answer to dwindling gas reserves. They said he could make a million in the next six months, though it would definitely limit his availability as a crimefighter.

Mouse was disappointed that their band of superheroes was splitting up, but he refused to dwell on it. They were his friends and he wanted nothing but good things for them. Plus he knew that if a dastardly criminal was to launch a sinister plan, all it would take was a phone call to re-assemble the mighty Z-List.

He listened to his headmaster, Mr Peach, as he launched into a speech on the subject of bravery, and raised his head to the back of the hall, where Mum and Dad both stood. Well, Mum was sitting comfortably, while Dad raced up and down, rounding up Dean, Roger, Clark, Peter and Bruce as they created mayhem.

Things had been different in their house since Dad had come home. Mum had done a lot more sitting down, and Dad . . . he hadn't. He'd cooked and cleaned and washed and ironed and swept out animal cages and . . . well, you get the idea, don't you?

Mum had laid down the law in a series of late-night loooong conversations. There hadn't been any shouting, not that Mouse had heard, but Dad was under no illusion that he was on trial. One false step and he would be disappearing again, at Mum's insistence this time.

Dad had decided to take a break from being a professional magician for a while, staying at home with the boys instead. Mouse was relieved to have him there, loved watching him enthrall his brothers by making Frederico appear mysteriously from tins of soup and packets of rice.

Mum, meanwhile, had taken advantage of an unexpected job offer from school.

They needed someone to run the office and keep the teaching staff in order. Who better than Mum? One bit of lip from anyone and she fixed them with her best Lady Lollipop stare. No one messed with a superhero. No one.

She hadn't give up her role as lollipop lady, either. There was no way Mum was going to walk away from the scene of her greatest battle. It was *her* crossing, and no one was taking it away from her.

She'd return from work at the end of each day tired but

content, sipping a tea as Mouse helped Dad turn the settee into a bed.

'Makes a change for you to be sleeping here at night instead of during the day, doesn't it?' Mouse had joked one evening.

'No more afternoon naps, son. I promised your mum, and I promise you too. No more snoozing.' Dad smiled embarrassedly and pulled Mouse into a hug, before apologising for the millionth time.

'You don't have to say sorry to me again, Dad. Another couple of years and you'll be able to stop saying it to Mum too.'

As Mouse watched his dad busying himself, he reckoned things might just work out, that they might even be better than they were before. If *he* could forgive Dad, then hopefully soon Mum would be able to, too.

Back in the school hall, Mr Peach was continuing with the compliments.

'The dictionary tells us that a hero is a person who is admired for their courage, outstanding achievements, or noble qualities. Can you see anyone in this room who fits that description?'

Hundreds of hands pointed in Mouse and the other Z-Listers' direction. Well, apart from the hands attached to Masher Milner, Saliva Shreeve and Bunions Bootle, who pointed at themselves.

Mouse didn't care what they thought, especially as they seemed to be staying away from him. It was still an amazing moment, one he would carry around for the rest of his life.

He stood on stage, in classic superhero pose – legs apart, chest puffed out, hands on hips. He felt a hundred metres tall.

It didn't matter that his towel, goggles and trunks were hung neatly in his wardrobe. It didn't matter that his costume today consisted solely of his drab, boring school uniform. Sometimes, Mouse thought with a smile, you don't need a cape to make you super . . .

The End (... for now ...)

Acknowledgements...

If you helped, encouraged and made cups of tea for me while I wrote this book, then thank you. If you're lucky, I'll make you a brew soon too. Maybe.

It would be terribly rude if I didn't thank all the caped crusaders at Orion Children's Books, in particular, Jenny Glencross on her last mission before swapping fighting crime for wiping bottoms.

Huge ta's also to Fiona Kennedy, Nina Douglas, Jennie Skinner, Jo Rose, Helen Thomas (Welcome!!) and all the sales bods who work bloomin' hard and never get the superhero status they deserve.

Mahoosive thank-you's to Jodie, Jane and Emily at United Agents, the Booksellers Crow for running the greatest bookshop on the planet, and my undying respect to Sara Ogilvie who always brings Storey Street magnificently to life.

To all my pals in Sarf East London, I miss you, but as always the biggest medals need to be pinned on the chests of Laura, Albie, Elsie and Stan, who do a super job of putting up with me. If you need me, I'll be in the shed.

The Shed, Hebden Bridge,
October 2015